"I Don't Remember Accepting Your Apology,"

James said.

"Well, do so, because storing up your grievances will give you ulcers and no friends."

"I do not hoard grievances!"

"Good. Then you won't have any problem accepting my apology."

"I'm not so sure about this fancy method of fighting of yours.... What do I get out of it?"

"The warm feeling of having done the right thing?" Her voice sounded husky in her own ears, and she hoped he hadn't heard. It would be humiliating if he were to notice her growing fascination with him.

"Wrong," he said succinctly. "I am not the least bit motivated by the glow of moral rectitude. I want a more tangible reward."

"Such as?" Elspeth asked cautiously, not liking the wicked smile curving his firm lips.

"The possibilities are endless. Let me think about it and I'll let you know."

Dear Reader:

Welcome! You hold in your hand a Silhouette Desire—your ticket to a whole new world of reading pleasure.

A Silhouette Desire is a sensuous, contemporary romance about passions, problems and the ultimate power of love. It is about today's woman—intelligent, successful, giving—but it is also the story of a romance between two people who are strong enough to follow their own individual paths, yet strong enough to compromise, as well.

These books are written by, for and about every woman that you are—wife, mother, sister, lover, daughter, career woman. A Silhouette Desire heroine must face the same challenges, achieve the same successes, in her story as you do in your own life.

The Silhouette reader is not afraid to enjoy herself. She knows when to take things seriously and when to indulge in a fantasy world. With six books a month, Silhouette Desire strives to meet her many moods, but each book is always a compelling love story.

Make a commitment to romance—go wild with Silhouette Desire!

Best,

Isabel Swift
Senior Editor & Editorial Coordinator

JUDITH McWILLIAMS
Reluctant Partners

Silhouette Desire

Published by Silhouette Books New York
America's Publisher of Contemporary Romance

With thanks to Mark Hutter,
a cordwainer extraordinaire with a knack
for making the past come alive,
and the Corning-Painted Post Historical Society,
who so ably maintains the Benjamin Patterson Inn
in its eighteenth-century form.

 SILHOUETTE BOOKS
300 East 42nd St., New York, N.Y. 10017

ISBN: 0-373-05441-6

First Silhouette Books printing August 1988

All the characters in this book are fictitious. Any
resemblance to actual persons, living or dead, is
purely coincidental.

Printed in the U.S.A.

Books by Judith McWilliams

Silhouette Desire
Reluctant Partners #441

Silhouette Romance
Gift of the Gods #479

JUDITH McWILLIAMS

began to enjoy romances while in search of the proverbial happily ever after. But she always found herself rewriting the endings, and eventually the beginnings, of the books she read. Then her husband finally suggested that she write one of her own, and she's been doing so ever since. A former teacher with four children, Judith has traveled the country extensively with her husband and has been greatly influenced by those experiences. But while not tending the garden of their upstate New York home, or caring for family, Judy does what she enjoys most—writing.

One

Grown women don't cry over something as trivial as not getting a job." Elspeth Fielding grumbled, but there was a curious lack of conviction in her voice. She'd been so sure that job was hers and instead...

She tightened her grip on her bulging sack of groceries as the elevator came to a jerky stop on the eleventh floor. The doors slid open and she slowly walked down the hallway toward her friend's apartment. For the first time since she'd arrived in New York City two days ago, Elspeth wished she'd opted to stay in a hotel. There she could have given way to the unhappiness overwhelming her. Instead, she was going to have to hide her feelings behind the polite facade demanded of a houseguest.

She stopped in front of Claudia's door, precariously shifted the groceries and groped in her purse for the key. Finally locating it at the bottom, she pulled it out and promptly dropped it. Her instinctive grab for the key

tipped the bag forward, sending several oranges career-
ing onto the floor.

"This most definitely is not my day," she muttered in
exasperation as she knelt to pick them up.

To her surprise, the apartment door swung open.

"Elspeth! What on earth are you doing down there?"
Claudia Vinton automatically reached for an orange lying
at her feet.

"Practicing begging on bended knee." Elspeth got up
and followed Claudia into the spacious apartment. "It's
the only thing I didn't try during the interview."

"I take it it didn't go well?"

"It didn't go, period." Elspeth set the sack on the
kitchen counter and automatically began to unpack the
food. "Apparently, the job market for reporters is so
tight it squeaks. 'Novice reporters are simply not being
added to the staff,'" she said, quoting the editor she'd
talked to.

"But you aren't a novice," Claudia protested. "You've
been working on a paper for eleven years."

"My dear Miss Vinton." Elspeth lifted her chin and
stared down her small nose in an excellent imitation of
the interviewing editor. "According to Ms. Shakely,
eleven years on a small weekly is not what it takes to
convince her that I have any skills in reporting."

"Ms. Shakely sounds like an arrogant snob! News is
news. The only difference is that New York City's is
usually more depressing."

"Snob or not, I'm afraid that she's got a point." Elspeth sighed despondently. "I must be the only reporter
looking for a job whose clips include interviews titled
'Vegetables of Unusual Size' or 'Nature's Own Pump-
kinhead'."

"Well, if she didn't like your background, why'd she invite you in for an interview?"

"She said she agreed to talk to me as a matter of courtesy because I had worked for the paper when I first got out of college."

"She may call it courtesy. I call it sadism! Getting your hopes up and then telling you they aren't hiring."

"But she didn't exactly say that." Elspeth ran her fingers through her short auburn curls in frustration. "What she actually said was that while she might find a place for a really promising reporter, my background didn't convince her I qualified."

"Well, that's her loss. What about the other papers?"

"Flat turndowns." Elspeth put the last of the groceries away and, extracting a cold soda from the refrigerator, took a long satisfying swallow. "As hot as it is out there, it's hard to believe that it's late September."

"And getting later by the minute." Claudia wandered into the living room and flopped down on the cream velvet sofa.

Elspeth followed. Kicking off her good Italian heels, she sat down on the chair across from Claudia and propped her feet up on the tiled coffee table.

"Is there some significance in that cryptic statement?" Elspeth asked, surfacing from her disappointment long enough to take a good look at her friend. Claudia looked tense and nervous, which was a complete departure from the aura of calm competence she normally exuded. "And now that I think about it, what are you doing home from work at two-thirty on a weekday?"

"Hiding," Claudia said seriously, "and for God's sake don't answer the phone if it rings. I don't think he's got my number, but I don't want to risk it."

"He?"

"James Murdoch, our literary agency's bright, shining star who is about to go nova."

"*The* James Murdoch? Master of the thriller? I didn't know your agency represented him. You've never mentioned him before."

"That's because I've never had anything to do with him before. I'm a very junior partner, and that only recently. Murdoch is the agency's bread and butter so my esteemed senior partner handles him himself. Unfortunately, Mr. Collins left three weeks ago on a two-month vacation and I'm stuck with Murdoch."

"I take it he's difficult?"

"Not normally, which was why Mr. Collins blithely sailed off to Europe and left me in charge. Usually Murdoch is an exemplary client. He never misses a deadline, his work's spectacular and all the agency has to do is prise his royalties out of his publisher."

"So what happened to change this ideal state of affairs? Did he decide he fancied you?"

"No." For a second Claudia looked disappointed. "He's all business in his dealings with me. Not even so much as a suggestive remark. No, the problem is that after twelve incredibly successful thrillers he wants to write a family saga set against the backdrop of the Revolutionary War."

"Rather a change of pace," Elspeth mused. "Why?"

"I don't know. He wouldn't say. He also wouldn't listen when I tried to point out all the very sound financial reasons why he should keep churning out thrillers. He just said he already had more money than he could ever spend and that he wasn't asking me for approval. Mr. Collins is going to come unglued when he finds out," she added morosely.

"You didn't tell him?"

"What would be the point?" She shrugged. "Mr. Collins has no more leverage over Murdoch than I do. Besides, his wife would never forgive me if I ruined the first vacation they've had in eighteen years. I just keep hoping that if I humor Murdoch, he'll come to his senses and give up this idea."

"And you're planning on staying holed up here until he does?" Elspeth asked skeptically.

"No. Tempting as the idea is, I'm only avoiding him till I can figure out what to tell him about the interview."

"Wait a minute. I missed something. What interview? Is Murdoch giving an interview?"

"Don't I just wish he would. But he won't. He absolutely never talks to the press. I could get him on any talk show on TV, but will he appear? Oh, no, he—"

"The interview, Claudia, the interview."

"Yeah, the interview. She said she wanted to find herself."

"Well, I certainly hope she does. Then at least one of us wouldn't be lost," Elspeth said in exasperation. "Start over and this time throw in a few more facts."

"You want facts? I'll give you facts. One: James Murdoch is going to at least start this family saga of his no matter what I say. Two: in order to get a real feel for the revolutionary period he intends to do his research while living exactly as an aspiring middle-class Upstate New York farmer of the 1770s did. Three: to help him do said research he asked the agency, which loosely translated means me, to find him a combination housekeeper-secretary."

"Oh."

"Yes, oh." Claudia grimaced. "I've had ads in all the papers and you wouldn't believe the responses I've gotten. One woman said she'd do it if I could convince her parole officer to let her leave the area. Another one said she wanted a peaceful interlude to fully explore her past lives."

"Past lives?" Elspeth laughed.

"It isn't funny." Claudia wailed. "What am I going to tell Murdoch? He knew I was talking to another candidate this afternoon and I'm beginning to get the distinct feeling he thinks I'm stalling about finding him a housekeeper so he can't start his research. And if he believes that, he's liable to simply bypass me altogether and then I'll have lost what little chance I may have had of influencing him."

"You know, Claudia, I think we may be able to help each other out," Elspeth said slowly. "As a matter of fact, I think your James Murdoch could be the answer."

"Would you care to tell me the question?" Claudia asked dryly.

"In fact I'm sure of it." Elspeth's dark brown eyes brightened. "It's the perfect solution, Claudia. Absolutely perfect."

"Don't tell me. I don't want to know." Claudia noticed the gleam in her friend's eyes with a great deal of trepidation. Over the years Elspeth had drawn her into some pretty wild schemes and the really frightening part was that every single one of them had seemed quite reasonable at the time.

"Yes you do, because my idea not only will solve my problem, but it'll get James Murdoch off your back. I'll take the job as his secretary-housekeeper."

"You!" Claudia yelped.

"Yes, me. My shorthand's adequate and my typing's excellent."

"How's your stiff upper lip?" Claudia scoffed. "If you'll remember, I said he was planning on living as they did in colonial times."

Elspeth shrugged. "What's the big deal? Two hundred years ago everybody in the whole country was living like that. And how long can it take to research one book anyway?"

"He's tentatively allotted eight weeks for it."

"Two months?" Elspeth considered the idea. "I can take it. What's two months when it'll open up a whole new future for me?"

"Somehow my future seems to be closing in on me," Claudia said glumly. "Would you please tell me why on earth any woman who wasn't either desperate for money or a certified nut would even consider the idea?"

"As the means to an end." Elspeth gestured emphatically with her soda can. "It's very simple. Remember Ms. Shakely said that a place could be found for the right person, but that eleven years on a weekly wasn't what it took to convince her I was the right person? So what would convince her? I'll tell you. An in-depth interview with the reclusive best-selling author, James Murdoch. Especially one that included the scoop that he's about to venture into new literary fields."

"No!" Claudia flatly vetoed the idea. "Absolutely, unequivocally no!"

"Why not?"

"Why not?" Claudia's voice rose. "I'll tell you why not—because James Murdoch would be livid when he found out I'd sicced a reporter on him. There's no telling how he'd react and frankly, I'm not all that keen to find out."

"Good Lord, Claudia, credit me with a little sense. I'm not going to tell the guy I'm a friend of yours. You can simply give me the name of one of the papers you advertised in and I'll say I answered the ad. He'll have no reason to suspect otherwise. There's nothing to tie me to you. We don't have any mutual friends in New York City and I've never visited you at work, so no one there could tell him we were college roommates. And I have no intention of dashing off some slick, sleazy piece. First, I'll get to know him. Then I'll do a well-written, well-developed interview."

"The publicity would be great. Especially with him suddenly changing the focus on his writing," Claudia murmured thoughtfully. "But even so..."

"Suppose I were to promise to get his okay on what I wrote before I took it to Ms. Shakely?"

"And, if he says no, you'll just drop the whole thing?" Claudia asked skeptically.

"If he says no, I'm going to try to make him change his mind." Elspeth's delicate features set in determination. "But I give you my word, I will publish nothing unless he agrees to it."

"Elspeth..." Claudia said slowly. "If you want to work in New York City so badly, why don't I call some of my contacts in publishing and see if they have anything open?"

"Thanks for the offer, Claudia, but I want to be an investigative reporter. On a top-notch newspaper. And I am going to. No matter what it takes," she vowed.

"All right." Claudia threw up her hands in defeat. "I'll go along with it."

"You won't be sorry," Elspeth assured her.

"I already am. Just remember what you promised."

* * *

Elspeth rubbed her damp palms down over her soft grey corduroy slacks and glanced nervously around the lobby of the Albany airport. The instructions that James Murdoch had given Claudia when she'd called him the previous week to tell him that she'd hired a housekeeper had been very specific. Elspeth was to fly to Albany the following Wednesday on the 2:15 flight, where he'd meet her and drive her north to his farm near Saratoga Springs. But where was he? Her anxious gaze swept the rapidly thinning crowd. There was no one who even vaguely resembled the picture she'd studied on the dust jacket of his latest book.

There was undoubtedly a very simple explanation for his not being here to meet her. She tried to calm her incipient fears that somehow he'd discovered what she intended to do and in retaliation had decided to stand her up. He was probably working and had simply lost track of the time. Sooner or later, he'd remember that he was supposed to be picking up his new housekeeper. In the meantime there was nothing for her to do but wait. Elspeth pulled the luggage cart which held her two large suitcases and a small cardboard box of writing supplies over to the row of orange plastic chairs lining one side of the lobby and sat down.

Idly, she watched as, one by one, her fellow passengers were met and left. Nearly forty-five minutes later, the lobby was virtually deserted except for an overweight businessman in an ill-fitting three-piece suit who was covertly eyeing her. Ignoring him, Elspeth once again scanned the room. She tensed as she looked through the large plate-glass windows and caught sight of a man hurrying toward the entrance. She squinted, trying to make out his features. A burst of excitement surged through her as she recognized him. It was James Murdoch.

Elspeth watched intently as he entered the lobby and turned toward the ticket desk. Her eyes measured the breadth of his shoulders beneath the pale blue knit of his shirt and then lingered on the impressive swell of his biceps before slipping lower, down over his hips and thighs.

She ran the tip of her tongue over her suddenly dry lips, frowning as the sound of her accelerated heartbeat echoed in her ears. She dismissed her uncharacteristic reaction as nerves. And heaven knew she had ample reason to be nervous. She had so little practice with either acting or deception and so much depended on her being able to carry off this masquerade.

Her precarious self-possession took another blow as she saw the clerk behind the ticket counter gesture toward her. Blindly, she stared down at the grey tiled floor and frantically tried to decide what a normal housekeeper would do. Wait for him to come to her? Go to meet him? Smile at him? The question became moot as his large sneaker-clad feet suddenly appeared in her line of vision.

Elspeth forced her gaze upwards along the length of his snugly fitting jeans, over his flat stomach, up past a heavily muscled chest and over a large nose, to drop into a fathomless pair of cerulean blue eyes. Mesmerized, she watched the shimmering silver lights radiating from their black irises.

"Elspeth Fielding?" The husky timbre of his voice sliced through her absorption. "I'm sorry you had to wait. There was an accident on the thruway and I stopped to help."

Scrambling for even a fraction of her normal social competence, Elspeth hastily got to her feet and accepted his outstretched hand. His fingers closed gently around hers and her flesh tingled where his callused skin touched hers. Ignoring the unexpected sensation, she said, "I hope no one was hurt, Mr. Murdoch?"

"James will suffice, and he wasn't hurt much. Only a few broken bones."

"Only?"

"Swerving at seventy miles an hour to avoid a deer could have been the last thing he ever did. Fortunately, he was wearing a seat belt," he replied absently, his attention focused on her slight figure.

What was he thinking? Elspeth tried to identify the emotions passing through his eyes, but she found it impossible.

"You aren't at all what I expected," he finally said.

"I'm a little frayed around the edges. I'm a very bad flyer," Elspeth offered.

"You look frayed straight through," he said bluntly. "But that wasn't what I meant. I was expecting someone with a little more—" He gestured vaguely with one large hand.

Elspeth stared blankly at him, uncertain of his meaning. "Could you be a little more explicit?"

"How about I was expecting a St. Bernard and I seem to have gotten a greyhound? And a miniature one at that. Elspeth, did Miss Vinton fully explain this job to you? Keeping house in colonial times involved a lot of hard physical labor. You simply don't look strong enough to do it."

"I'm a lot stronger than I look and, besides, haven't you ever heard that wiry people wear the best?"

"I've heard lots of things in my time. That's not to say I believe them," he replied dryly.

"You can believe me when I say that I can do the job."
She tried to sound extremely confident. It would be the
final irony if James Murdoch rejected her for what he
thought was her own good.

"Why are you—" He paused, a thoughtful expression suddenly darkening his eyes. "You wouldn't happen to be an aspiring author who's just written the next
great American novel would you? A novel you're going
to try to convince me to help you get published?"

"Of course not!"

"You're sure, Elspeth Fielding?" His expression was
almost indulgent. "If I'm right, this is the time to tell me
because I give you fair warning, I won't be lied to."

Frantically, Elspeth weighed her options. Should she
risk making a clean breast of everything now and hope
he'd agree to an interview? But why would he? There was
a big difference between an unknown housekeeper who
wanted him to help her get a book published and one who
wanted to delve into his personal and professional life for
the purpose of furthering her own career. For the first
time, she experienced a twinge of guilt over what she was
planning to do, but she immediately suppressed it. The
benefits weren't all on her side, she salved her conscience. As Claudia had said, publicity sold books.

No, Elspeth quickly decided. This was not the time to
confess. Not while he was already worried about her
ability to cope with colonial-style housekeeping. And
especially not while they were still at the airport where he
could so easily send her back to New York City.

"I've never written a novel in my life, nor do I have the
slightest intention of ever doing so," she stated emphatically.

"Then why are you so hell-bent on taking a job that's clearly going to tax your physical strength?" He ran impatient fingers through his short black hair.

"Because of the excellent pay you're offering." Elspeth decided that painting herself as mercenary would be a good idea. It might stop him from probing for other, more damning motives.

"The money's important to you?" He eyed her narrowly.

"Money is always important when you haven't got any." She managed to give the impression of near poverty without telling an outright lie.

"And why don't you have any money, Elspeth Fielding? By your age a woman's usually either married or firmly established in a career." He frowned. "There isn't an irate husband somewhere in the background, is there?"

"Good God, no! I've never been married. And for your information, thirty-three isn't all that old," she added tartly.

"Old enough to have started to climb the ladder of success. What have you been doing with your life?"

"Nothing that would interest you." She tried one last time to put him off.

"No," he said slowly, "you're wrong. I'm beginning to find you very interesting."

Oh, great! Just what she needed. Somehow, she'd never expected that a successful man like James Murdoch would pay any attention to his housekeeper. But then he was turning out to be unexpected all around, she thought uneasily. It was obvious that she was going to have to tell him something about her background. But what? She sifted through the possibilities and decided on the truth. Or, at least, part of it. Lies were too chancy. If she told very many she could easily forget what she'd said and, if he caught her in one, it could put an end to all her plans.

Trying for a casual tone, she said, "There's no mystery involved. A few months after I graduated from college, my father had a massive heart attack and died. I was a late addition to their lives, and my mother was sixty-seven at the time. I was worried about her living upstate by herself while I worked in New York City so I resigned from my job and moved home."

"You have a college degree?" His voice hardened slightly.

"Uh-huh. In middle European history," she elaborated, too relieved that he hadn't asked what kind of job she'd resigned from to wonder why he'd picked up on her having graduated from college. After all, in this day and age, college degrees were a dime a dozen.

"I see. And what happened when you moved back home?"

"Nothing. Mother and I lived together quite happily until last May when..." Her expression became bleak as she relived the horror she'd felt when she'd gone to waken her mother one morning and found her dead.

"When?" James prompted.

"When she died," Elspeth said starkly.

Unexpectedly, his large hand closed comfortingly over her shoulder. "And suddenly you found you'd lost your purpose in life." His insight surprised her. "And your appetite, too, from the looks of you."

"Being thin is fashionable." She took exception to the implied criticism.

"You aren't thin; you're skinny. But why aren't you looking for a job with a future in it? Miss Vinton did tell you that this job was strictly temporary, didn't she?"

"Temporary and well paid," Elspeth replied, trying to reinforce the straightforward, pragmatic motive. "Two months with you and I'll have enough saved to take my time about finding something else. I'm sure this will work out well for me," she said, hoping with all her heart it was true. She simply had to get an interview with him. Everything depended on it.

"Do you?" He looked skeptical.

"I see no reason why it shouldn't. I may not fit your preconceived image of a colonial housekeeper, but I'm here and I'm willing, which is a big advantage," she pointed out.

"Hmm. I take it I'm to think of you as a bird in the hand." His eyes dropped to study the slight curve of her small breasts.

She was shocked to feel a bright curl of excitement run through her, causing the tips of her breasts to harden until they pushed provocatively against her thin grey sweater. Easy girl, Elspeth told herself. James Murdoch might be setting himself up as a backwoods farmer, but according to the extensive research she'd done the previous week, eight years ago he'd been moving in some pretty sophisticated circles in California. He was obviously a master at the art of the double entendre.

If that's what his comment had been. She was suddenly uncertain. She simply didn't have sufficient experience to parry his remarks effectively. Her best bet would undoubtedly be to respond to exactly what he said and studiously ignore any hidden meanings, she decided.

"Why don't we compromise, James? I'll try the job and you write to that Miss Vinton who hired me and ask her to keep an eye out for a strapping young woman who tosses weights around," she said with a touch of acid, secure in the knowledge that Claudia would file his request in the wastebasket where it belonged.

"Instead of sharp words?" His lips twitched. "Very well, Elspeth, you may try the job, provided you promise you'll let me know if it gets to be too much for you. And in exchange, I promise you a kill fee if I decide to replace you," he said gruffly.

"Agreed." Elspeth tried not to let the feeling of exultant triumph which welled up in her show in her voice. She had passed the first obstacle. She was on her way toward a bright, shining future.

"Here, you take this." He picked up her small cardboard box, handed it to her and then lifted her two large suitcases. "You certainly believe in coming prepared. The average colonial housewife was lucky if she had three dresses and a spare chemise."

"I sure hope this book of yours doesn't have any espionage in it." She tried to match her steps to his long-legged stride.

"Why?" He slowed his pace slightly.

"Because with your fetish for accuracy, I can just visualize the pair of us scaling the fence around a military base to get the feel of spying," she said tartly.

"Skinny as you are, I could probably just slip you under it." He grinned at her.

Elspeth blinked under the impact of his gleaming smile. Why was she reacting so uncharacteristically to this man? she wondered uneasily. But before she could reach any kind of conclusion, her speculations were interrupted by a buxom, middle-aged woman who, with a squeal of delighted recognition, planted herself directly in front of James.

"You're James Murdoch! I know you are," she insisted, as if afraid he might deny it.

"So I am." His voice was even, but Elspeth was so close to him she could feel the tension tightening his muscles. Curiously she glanced at him, amazed to see a faint reddish tinge coloring his neck. He was embarrassed, she realized with a sudden flash of insight. And that seemed a very strange reaction for a man who, according to the old gossip columns she'd unearthed, had positively wallowed in public adulation for the first three years of his career. Why had he changed? she wondered. She didn't know, but she fully intended to find out. The answer would add depth to the interview she planned.

"I've read every one of your books and I just love them," the woman gushed. "They give me goose bumps. Can I have your autograph?" She shoved a scrap of paper and a pen at him. "My name's Winifred."

Quickly, he scrawled something and handed it back to her.

"Thank you so much, Mr. Murdoch." The woman beamed happily at him.

"You're welcome." He gave her a harassed smile, and with a nod at Elspeth, slipped through the lobby doors and headed toward the parking lot.

"Does that kind of thing happen often?" Elspeth asked as she hurried after him.

"No, thank God!"

"Don't you enjoy being recognized?"

"I enjoy people liking my work, but so many of them don't seem to be able to separate me from the fiction I write. I always feel as if I'm a disappointment to them."

"Winifred certainly wasn't disappointed." Elspeth forced a light response. What she really wanted to do was to follow up with more questions about his rather surprising admission, but she resisted the impulse. This wasn't the time to risk reanimating his suspicions about her motives for having taken the job.

Two

_____

"Seat belt fastened?" James asked, waiting for her affirmative answer before pulling smoothly into the heavy traffic on the road leading out of the airport.

Elspeth studied him surreptitiously. A shiver trickled down her spine at the feeling of power his personality projected. She was going to have to tread very carefully. There was a basic shrewdness about James Murdoch that made deceiving him a risky proposition.

She blinked as he suddenly pulled off the road into a parking lot. Shaking off her thoughts, she looked around. They were in front of a large motel.

"I thought we were going up to your farm." She tried to ignore her fear that he was about to leave her here for the night and send her back to New York City in the morning. He'd said she could try the job, she reminded herself, and everything she'd been able to discover about James Murdoch so far highlighted the fact that he was a man of his word. He had the kind of integrity you could bruise yourself on.

"We are." He cut the engine. "Just as soon as you have dinner."

"They served a meal on the plane." Elspeth made no move to get out.

"Which you didn't eat," he stated with absolute certainty.

"What makes you say that?" she asked idly, her attention focused on the way the red neon light of the motel's sign was reflected in his eyes. In the dimness they seemed to glow with an incandescent flame. With the fires of hell. She shivered at the images her fanciful imagining was creating.

"Come on. Let's go," James ordered.

She was about to tell him she wasn't the least bit hungry, when it suddenly struck her that a leisurely dinner with him would be an excellent opportunity to start gathering information for her interview. It was an opportunity she'd be foolish to pass up because once they reached their destination, she probably wouldn't see him all that much. He'd undoubtedly rented some huge, rambling eighteenth-century farmhouse where, as his housekeeper, she'd have quarters off the kitchen while he worked and lived in the main part of the house. Eating a meal she didn't want seemed a small price to pay for the privilege of actually taking the first step on her journey toward a career as an investigative reporter.

"Dinner sounds great." Her enthusiasm was reflected in her voice and James gave her an indulgent smile as he climbed out of the truck.

Elspeth waited a second to see if he was going to come over and open her door, but he merely leaned against the front fender on the driver's side waiting for her.

Shrugging, Elspeth opened her own door and got out. She wondered if his pragmatic approach was due to the fact that she was the housekeeper, or if he believed in treating women as equals and ignoring small courtesies, or, perhaps, whether he simply didn't know what was expected of a gentleman.

She considered her last idea as she walked beside him across the parking lot. She knew from her research that he came from a very poor family, but she also knew that after his second bestseller he'd moved freely in the upper levels of both American and European society. In fact, eight years ago he'd been living with a gorgeous starlet who'd later married a French count. Surely she'd tried to teach him what was expected of a gentleman.

Elspeth glanced at James, her eyes lingering on the uncompromising line of his jaw. Just because the starlet had tried to teach him was no reason to assume he'd tried to learn, she conceded.

Stumbling slightly when she unexpectedly stepped on a small stone, Elspeth instinctively grabbed for the nearest support—James. A tremor of uncertainty chased over her as she felt the rough hair on his forearm with her soft fingertips.

"Excuse me," she muttered, hastily withdrawing her hand.

"No problem." James gave her a sharp glance. "Are you all right?"

"Of course I'm all right." She ignored the strange sensation touching him had provoked. "I'm simply not used to rushing across parking lots."

"Why didn't you tell me to slow down?" he asked reasonably.

"Because you weren't going too fast for me to keep up with. At least you wouldn't have been if I hadn't stepped on a rock." She bounded up the steps to the restaurant, determined to present an image of vibrant energy.

Not waiting for him to open the door, she pushed it open and stepped inside. The heat felt good against her chilled skin and she rubbed her hands over her arms while she waited for the hostess to appear.

"You should be wearing a jacket." James frowned at her thin gray sweater. "Haven't you got one?"

"Got one?" Elspeth repeated as she tried to decide how deeply to play her poverty-stricken role. Not that deeply, she decided. "Of course I have a jacket. It's in one of my suitcases. I came prepared for every eventuality." Except, perhaps, you, she added mentally.

"You won't need all that stuff," James said.

About to ask him what he meant, she was distracted when the hostess approached them. Elspeth watched as the woman's gaze slid uninterestedly over her to land on James. A slow, seductive smile suddenly curved the woman's lips into a provocative pout as she studied him through what had to be artificial lashes. Honestly, Elspeth thought, giving the woman an annoyed glare, this wasn't some two-bit truck stop where anything went. This was the main dining room of a highly respected motel chain.

As if that fact had suddenly occurred to their hostess, too, the woman rearranged her features into a more professional smile and with a throatily murmured "Follow me," led them toward an empty table at the back of the room.

There was nothing professional, though, about the undulating movement of the woman's hips, Elspeth noted with frank envy. If she tried to walk like that, she'd probably throw her back out.

Elspeth waited a fraction of a second for James to pull out her chair and when he didn't, she seated herself.

"Would you care for a drink?" the hostess purred.

"Elspeth?" James glanced at her.

She shook her head. Alcohol on top of an almost sleepless night would probably send her straight to sleep.

"Nothing, thank you." James's words were definitely a dismissal, which the woman accepted in good part. Handing them each a menu, she said, "Your waitress will be here to take your order shortly."

Elspeth watched her walk away and then turned back to find James watching her.

"What's wrong?" she asked.

"That should be my line. For a second there you looked like a kid with your nose pressed up against the candy store window."

"Please." Ruefully, she shook her head. "At my age I like to think I'm a little more sophisticated than that."

"You might be many things, Elspeth Fielding, but sophisticated doesn't appear to be one of them. What's wrong?" He returned tenaciously to the subject.

About to put him off, Elspeth suddenly decided to answer him truthfully. Maybe her candor would nudge him into a few revelations of his own.

She leaned toward him and said, "Quite frankly, I'm consumed with envy at the way she moves. I tried to learn how to sway like that when I was a teenager and I simply looked like a little girl trying to walk in her mother's high heels."

Elspeth watched in fascination as dawning amusement lightened his eyes to sky blue.

"If it's any consolation to you, you don't look like a little girl. You may be on the puny side, but what there is of you is most definitely grown-up."

"Petite." She took exception to his choice of adjective. "Dogs are puny and I am not a dog."

"I certainly hope not, since a female dog is a bitch, isn't it?" James gave her a bland smile.

Inwardly, Elspeth winced, very much fearing that if James knew why she was here, he'd definitely think that she deserved the title. To her relief, the waitress arrived to rescue her from a conversation that was becoming more impossible by the second. Apparently, it was going to be a lot harder than she'd expected to maneuver him into making disclosures about himself.

"Are you ready to order?" The waitress gave them a cheerful smile.

"Yes, thank you." Elspeth smiled back. "I'll have the salad bar and coffee."

"What about a main course?" James asked.

Elspeth blinked, taken aback. She'd never had an escort question her choice of dinner before.

"The salad bar's fine," she assured him.

"Salad is for rabbits. People need protein. Especially considering what you're going to be doing. Bring her a strip steak to go with the salad bar. I'll have the prime rib, rare, baked potato with butter and sour cream, asparagus with hollandaise sauce and coffee."

"Yes, sir." The woman hastily scribbled the order down. "And how would you like your steak, madam?" She turned to Elspeth.

About to deny vehemently any desire for a steak, Elspeth suddenly noticed the knowing gleam in the woman's eyes. Quite obviously, she'd put her own interpretation on what James expected her to be expending so much energy on. Ah, well, Elspeth consoled herself, Barbara Walters had probably had her share of embarrassing moments when she was starting out, too.

"Medium," she said, handing her menu back to the waitress who, with one last speculative look, left.

"Don't sulk," James ordered.

"I wasn't sulking!" Her head shot up. "If you must know I was embarrassed." Annoyance jerked the truth out of her.

"Embarrassed?" Thoughtfully, he drummed his fingers on the gleaming white tablecloth. Mesmerized, she watched their rhythmic movement. He had strong hands. Powerful, like the rest of his body.

"Now, why would you be embarrassed?" He studied her. "Elspeth, you aren't worried I'll make you pay for your dinner, are you?"

"Well..." she hedged, not wanting to mention the real cause of her embarrassment. If he'd missed the innuendo in his words, it would undoubtedly be best to leave it that way. She didn't want to start him thinking of her in sensual terms. It would be far better for her plans if he thought of her as his sexless housekeeper. She firmly ignored the regret which filtered through her mind.

James reached out and gently squeezed her hand, which was lying on the table. Tiny pinpricks darted through her fingers, making her flesh tingle with vibrant life. Elspeth swallowed uneasily, not understanding her reaction to his casual touch. It made no sense. He wasn't trying to seduce her. He was offering her comfort in much the same way he might offer it to his ninety-year-old grandmother.

To her relief, he leaned back in his chair and said, "In case Miss Vinton didn't mention it, this job includes room and board. As far as I'm concerned, anything you eat is board and, therefore, my responsibility."

"Thank you," Elspeth said hollowly, beginning to see some very real pitfalls in the penurious role she'd so impulsively adopted. Not the least of which were the three major credit cards in her purse, as well as the two one-hundred-dollar bills she had pinned to the inside of her bra for emergencies. Not only was she going to have to keep them well hidden, but she wasn't going to be able to buy anything. When Shakespeare had said, "what a tangled web we weave when first we practice to deceive," he'd sure known what he'd been talking about. She sighed.

"There's no reason to be embarrassed," he said. "Almost everyone has this problem at some time in their life. I can remember when I didn't have the price of a square meal."

"Oh?" Elspeth murmured, hoping to get him talking. "When was that?"

"When I was young and stupid."

"Young, maybe, but stupid . . ." She eyed him doubtfully.

"Oh, but I was." He grimaced. "Young and stupid and without even the saving grace of idealism. Now, shall we pay a visit to this salad bar you're so keen on?"

"Sure." Elspeth stifled the questions she wanted to ask. There would be time over the next two months to delve into how he viewed his past.

Once back at their table, she gamely began to munch her way through a meal she didn't want. She found it rough going. By the time her steak arrived, she was more than ready to quit, but she didn't want to waste her energy and James's patience arguing over something as trivial as food.

"Tell me about this colonial farm you've been living at," she asked.

"I haven't actually been living there. I've been staying at the Hilton in Saratoga Springs while I was waiting for

Miss Vinton to come up with a housekeeper. Now that she has..." He gave her a doubtful look that made Elspeth very uneasy. "I checked out of the hotel this morning. Tomorrow I can begin my research in earnest."

"Of course." Elspeth gave him what she hoped was a confident smile. Unfortunately, a huge yawn caught her unawares in the middle of it, spoiling the effect.

"You're going to be a natural." James chuckled. "The colonists were pretty much early to bed and early to rise."

"Sorry," she muttered. "I was a little nervous last night and couldn't sleep."

"Then if you're through playing with your food, let's go. We've got a two-hour drive in front of us before you can go to bed."

"Certainly." Elspeth stood up and followed him across the dining room toward the cashier, not totally disappointed by her fledgling attempts to surreptitiously interview him. Even though she hadn't learned anything she didn't already know, he had made several comments which had given her intriguing glimpses into his thought processes. With luck, she'd be able to follow up on them later.

"Here." He turned from paying the bill and shoved a small white sack at her.

She automatically accepted it. "What is it?"

"Candy bars." He motioned her toward the door. "In case you get hungry later."

"Um, thank you." Elspeth was torn between feminine annoyance that he seemed to find her figure so lacking that he wanted to fatten her up and a strange feeling she couldn't quite identify about his attempts to look after her. It was not the reaction she was used to receiving from men. Her few dates back home in the village of Litton had been with men she'd known all her life. Men who knew that she was an intelligent, highly practical individual who was quite capable of handling anything that came her way.

Well, almost anything, she amended, her eyes lingering on the impressive width of James's shoulders as she followed him outside. She had the disquieting feeling that James Murdoch wasn't going to fit into any nice, neat little niche like most men she'd known. Instead, he seemed to be a swirling kaleidoscope of many things—the vast majority of which defied easy labeling.

But that was an advantage, she tried to convince herself as she climbed into the pickup truck. His complex personality would add depth and scope to her interview, making it more marketable. A spark of her original excitement flickered, only to be smothered by the feeling of guilt which engulfed her as her sack of candy bars crackled when she laid them on the seat beside her.

Telling herself she was being overly sensitive, that public figures were fair game for journalists, she leaned back against the seat and closed her eyes, intending only to rest them for a few minutes. But the warm darkness combined with the rhythmic movement of the truck soon sent her to sleep.

It wasn't until almost two and a half hours later that she was rudely awakened as she was violently flung against her seat belt.

"What's wrong?" she gasped. Fearfully, she glanced around, half expecting to find herself in the middle of a thruway accident. But they weren't even on the highway. She frowned in confusion at the massive oaks visible in the beam of the truck's headlights.

"That damn Wilder didn't deliver the gravel. Gravel I've already paid for."

"Gravel?" Her mind scrambled to make sense of his words.

"For filling in the potholes in the driveway." He put the truck in first and cautiously crept forward. "I should have checked on him this morning," James bit out, his tone not boding well for the absent Wilder.

Curiously, Elspeth peered into the darkness. "Look, James. Aren't they cute?" She gestured at the mother raccoon and two cubs standing poised at the side of the driveway with unfeigned enthusiasm.

"They're also wild animals and surprisingly intelligent. Stay away from them," he declared as the raccoons melted into the trees.

"The warning isn't necessary," she replied mildly. "I've spent most of my life in a small village and I know all about wild animals."

"Including the two-legged variety?" His grin was ghostly in the reflected light from the dashboard.

"The two-legged variety I've known haven't been very wild." Her voice was unconsciously wistful. "At least, not *interestingly* wild."

"Believe me, wildness palls pretty quickly when you have to live with it on a daily basis." James's voice was hard, and Elspeth wondered which of the many escapades her research had uncovered he was remembering.

"Tell me about this house you've rented," she said, hoping he'd get so used to her asking questions that he'd automatically answer them.

"Bought. It seemed simpler to buy than to have to keep getting permission from a landlord every time I wanted to do something."

No, he wouldn't like having to ask permission, Elspeth thought with a quick glance at his profile. From what she'd been able to find out, the role of supplicant was not one he'd played in a long time. She wondered what he would be like in that role. An image flashed through her mind of his lean features sharpened with passion, his eyes darkened by desire as he leaned over her. She clenched her teeth against the sudden tension that twisted through her abdomen.

"There it is." The object of her fantasy suddenly spoke, shattering the illusion, and in relief she turned in the direction he was pointing.

She saw a very small building illuminated in the bright beam of the headlights. Frowning, she squinted into the darkness behind it, trying to find the rambling colonial mansion of her imagination. It wasn't there.

"Where's the house?" she demanded.

"There." He gestured toward the tiny building.

"There?" Elspeth swallowed uneasily, rapidly reassessing the situation. It was one thing to contemplate staying with James Murdoch in a large house where their contact would be minimal and quite another to share this crackerbox with him. They'd be living on top of each other. All the easier to question him, she thought stoutly, trying to rally her flagging enthusiasm.

"You were expecting something bigger?" he guessed shrewdly.

"Well, yes," she admitted. "All the colonial homes I've known have been big, oversize things."

"They belonged to the upper classes. The houses that the aspiring middle-class farmers owned were quite small and usually torn down for their lumber when the farmer could afford something better. It was an incredible stroke of luck finding this one almost intact."

"Almost?" she repeated suspiciously.

"I had to have some missing shingles and floorboards replaced." He leaned toward her and Elspeth instinctively pressed back against her seat, but the faint aroma of his after-shave followed her, tugging at her senses.

"Excuse me," James murmured as he opened the glove compartment and pulled out a large flashlight.

"S'okay," she muttered, flexing her fingers to dispel the sudden longing to touch him.

"Come on. Let's go look things over. I left Wilder with a list of things to pick up in town and bring out to the house. Let's hope he was more attentive to those details than he was to the gravel."

Filled with a confused mixture of excitement and foreboding, Elspeth climbed out of the truck, shuddering as the chill October air sliced through her thin sweater.

"Brrr." She wrapped her arms around herself and hurried after the bobbing glare of the powerful flashlight.

"Why don't you unpack your jacket?" He played the beam over her shivering body.

"What's the point? We're going to be inside in a minute. At least we will be if you'd hurry up and unlock the door." She gestured toward the shiny padlock on the plain wooden door behind him. "You do have the key, don't you?"

"Of course. Here, hold this." He handed her the flashlight and then pulled a large key ring out of his pocket. Selecting the one he wanted, he unlocked the door and pushed.

It swung open with an eerie creak and Elspeth nervously peered over her shoulder into the pitch blackness.

"I don't know about this new book you've got planned, but this place would be a natural for one of those thrillers you write. Isolated, run-down, creaking," she added as the wind caught the door and swung it back and forth. "All we need is an ax-wielding maniac." She edged closer to him.

"The only ax around here belongs to me and I only become a maniac when meals aren't on time," he said dryly. "Now give me the light and stow the imagination."

"That's fine advice coming from a writer." She handed him the flashlight, for once grateful for his habit of not waiting for the woman to go first. Anything could be in that cabin, the lock notwithstanding.

"Imagination is grossly overrated." He stepped into the cabin with a confidence Elspeth envied.

She watched as he swung the beam of the flashlight around the small room, vaguely glad the lighting was so bad. She was positive she'd feel more up to coping with all this unrelieved primitive Americana after a good night's sleep.

Sleep? She blinked as the flashlight briefly illuminated a corner of the room, revealing one bed. Hastily, she bit back her instinctive protest. There had to be another bed, she assured herself. James Murdoch had been expecting a housekeeper. A stranger, not a lover.

"Hm." He walked over to the long wooden table in the middle of the room and shone the beam of the flashlight into the three cardboard boxes on it. "Wilder did some of the things he was supposed to," he mused. "These appear to be the cooking utensils and bedding I ordered."

"Maybe he couldn't find any gravel." Elspeth yawned, not really interested. Tomorrow was time enough to worry about the unknown Wilder's incompetence.

James ignored her, disappearing through the doorway to the left of the huge fieldstone fireplace which almost filled one entire wall of the cabin.

Elspeth cautiously made her way across the rough wooden floor after him. She had no desire to be left alone in the darkness. The cold darkness. She shivered convulsively. If anything, it was colder in here than outside.

She found James standing in the middle of the tiny lean-to attached to the back of the cabin, swearing steadily.

"Talk about lack of imagination!" she declared, taking exception to his vocabulary.

"Look at that." He played the light over the empty shelves.

"Look at what? There's nothing there."

"Precisely!"

"But there's supposed to be?" she hazarded a guess.

"Damn right, there's supposed to be! I told Wilder to buy food."

"He probably ran afoul of something out there." Elspeth peered apprehensively through the lean-to's one small window. "Like a bear or an escaped murderer." She swallowed nervously.

"The few bears around here are brown ones and they're only dangerous if you happen to get between them and their young. And as for an escaped murderer, would you stick around here if you'd managed to break out of jail?"

"Good point," she conceded around an enormous yawn.

"You're asleep on your feet, woman."

"Just getting into the spirit of things," she muttered. "As you pointed out, the colonists went to bed pretty early. And I'm beginning to see why." She glanced around the barren lean-to. "There was nothing else to do."

"It was because they got up at the crack of dawn," he insisted. "And we'll see about stocking these shelves first thing tomorrow."

Oh, goody, something to look forward to, she thought, but she left the words unsaid. James Murdoch was paying her well to put up with a few discomforts. And he didn't even know how well. She hugged the promise of her interview to herself, but, somehow, not even the thought of her bright future was sufficient to dispel the gloom.

"Come on, I'll take you up to your quarters."

"Up?" Elspeth queried as she trotted along behind him.

"Uh-huh." He crossed the main room and started up a steep set of stairs which she hadn't noticed in the darkness. "In a farmhouse of this type the farmer and his wife slept in the main room with the baby. Older kids slept in the loft, which is where I put you."

He paused at the top of the stairs and played the flashlight in all the corners.

Elspeth looked around, well pleased with her quarters. Although the room was barren, containing only a narrow wooden bed and a rickety-looking chest of drawers, the sloping roof gave it a cosy feeling and, more importantly, it was private.

"Very nice," she said. "As a matter of fact, it reminds me of summer camp."

"Probably Scout camp." He smiled at her. "Because you're turning out to be a pretty good one. If the physical labor just doesn't prove to be too much for you."

"If you'll bring up my case and point out the bathroom?" She changed the subject, refusing to allow him to dwell on her supposed shortcomings.

"The facilities are of the outdoor variety, about a hundred yards behind the house. And I'll get your cases, but you won't be needing them."

Elspeth's disbelief that he hadn't added a bathroom, no matter what he wanted to research, was quickly superseded by a sense of foreboding.

"Why won't I be needing them?" she asked suspiciously.

"Because you'll be wearing period costumes to help set the scene." He shone the flashlight over some shapeless garments hanging on pegs on the far wall. "I had the movie studio that's filming my latest book make up three sets of clothes. About what an aspiring middle-class farmer's wife would have."

"It's a good thing for you I was always a sucker for Halloween. And speaking of things that go bump in the night, may I borrow the flashlight to go to the john?"

"Sure, but wait till I get your cases from the truck. Tomorrow we'll locate the candles and things will be easier."

Than what? Elspeth thought grimly, watching him leave. It could be worse, she tried to tell herself. A lot worse. And there were compensations. She could work on her article up here in complete privacy. Absently, she sat down on the narrow bed, and then shot to her feet in surprise as it rustled beneath her.

"What on earth!" Cautiously she poked the bed with her hand and it rustled again. She squinted, trying to get a better look in the moonlight pouring in through the room's two small windows.

"What's wrong?" James reappeared at the top of the stairs.

"My bed talks."

"Talks?"

"Rustles. Like . . . like a pile of leaves."

"Oh, that." He set her two cases down in front of the chest of drawers and tossed her small cardboard box on top of it. "It's just the straw. For authenticity."

"I have a sneaking suspicion that's a phrase I'm going to come to hate. Why is rustling authentic?"

"Not the rustling. What causes it. The straw," he elaborated at her blank expression. "Farmers in the revolutionary period slept on mattresses stuffed with straw."

"If you already know that, then why are you sleeping on one? You *are* sleeping on one, too, aren't you?" she demanded.

"Of course I am. We're partners in this, Elspeth."

However reluctant that partnership may be on both sides, Elspeth thought, wondering for the first time if, perhaps, there weren't worse things in life than interviewing amateur gardeners.

"Poor Elspeth." James awkwardly patted her shoulder. "You're just tired. Things will look better in the morning."

"At least in the morning I'll be able to look," she snapped and immediately felt ashamed of herself. She'd agreed to this. No one had forced her into it.

"Sorry," she apologized. "You're right. I'm just a little tired. I think I'll turn in now. Good night."

"Good idea," he agreed. He gave her one last pat on the shoulder as he left—for all the world as if she were a stray puppy he'd found on his doorstep and wasn't quite certain what to do with, she thought in wry amusement.

Three

Elspeth muttered protestingly as the bright October sunlight streaming in through the bare windows seeped under her eyelids, nudging her awake. She tried to roll away from the persistent light, but her movement brought her into contact with the sharp end of a straw stem protruding through the mattress's thin cover.

"Damn!" she mumbled, forcing open eyelids that felt glued together. Wearily, she rubbed her forehead and sat up, grimacing at the rustling sound. She felt as if she should be going to bed, not getting up. She groaned as a series of sneezes suddenly shook her slender body. Oh, no! All she needed was for her usually dormant allergies to start acting up.

She pulled her legs up and rested her aching forehead on her knees. There had to be an easier way to break into journalism, she thought. It was a cinch there wasn't a harder way.

"Elspeth? Are you awake yet?" James's voice floated up the stairs. "We need to get moving. We're going after supplies, remember?"

"Com—" Her voice emerged as a hoarse croak. She swallowed and tried again. "I'll be down in a few minutes."

Her estimation of the time needed to dress turned out to be dismayingly accurate. With no bathroom, no water and no mirror there was no incentive to linger in her chilly attic.

"Good morning. How was sleeping on a straw mattress?" James subjected her to an intense scrutiny as she trailed down the stairs.

"Lovely," she lied with a bright smile which sat oddly on her red, swollen features.

"Lovely?" he repeated, slowly getting to his feet and walking toward her.

"What do you do for water around this place if you haven't got a bathroom?" she continued in the same determinedly bright voice.

"There's a well out behind the house," he answered absently, his attention clearly centered on her face.

"I guess I'll wash up, then, before we leave." She started toward the door, only to come to a precipitous halt as his large hand closed around her upper arm.

The warmth of his fingers left a burning imprint on her chilled skin and she shifted uneasily.

"You said you were in a hurry to leave." She tried to move away, but his fingers tightened like a manacle.

"Not that much of a hurry." He lightly brushed his fingertips across her swollen eyelids and then down over the tip of her reddened nose.

Tiny rivulets of sensation arced from his hand to her skin, leaving a strange tingling sensation in their wake.

"What happened?" he demanded. "When you went to bed last night your skin was a clear, creamy ivory. Now it's swollen with red blotches."

Clear, creamy ivory? The words echoed in her mind. Is that what he thought of her complexion or was it merely the writer in him, embellishing what he saw?

"Elspeth?" He gave her a gentle shake and she hastily brought her mind back to the present.

"Well..." She glanced up into his eyes, darkened to a bluish grey by whatever emotion was motivating his questions. His tone of voice suggested concern, but that concern could just as easily be worry over the fact that his research couldn't start today if she were sick, she reminded herself.

"Well what?"

"You have all the patience of a whistling tea kettle."

"And the persistence of the Internal Revenue. So save us both a lot of time and answer me."

"I don't have any makeup on this morning. Last night I did."

"Makeup wouldn't cover that. Damn it, woman, why won't you trust me?" His eyes gleamed briefly with what she suspected was hurt. The suspicion made her candid.

"It's not a question of trust, James. It's a question of survival."

"Survival?" He stared blankly at her.

"I need this job and you've already got some hare-brained notion that the only good housekeeper is one who looks like a Sumo wrestler."

James dropped her arm and she shivered as a sense of loss swept through her. She watched as he took a few steps across the room and turned to stare at her in frustration.

"Do I seem like such an ogre to you?"

"No," she answered honestly. "Simply a man who's single-minded to the point of fanaticism. I also have the sneaking suspicion that once you get an idea in your head it would take dynamite to get it out."

"That's not true!" He sounded shocked by her charge. "I'm very broad-minded."

"If you say so."

"And I promised you a kill fee if I sent you back," he reminded her.

"I neither want nor need your charity!"

"I think what you need is a doctor." He frowned at her.

Elspeth opened her mouth to deny it and promptly sneezed six times.

"It's only a slight flare-up of an allergy," she said when she could talk again. "Annoying, but hardly worth more than a passing 'too bad.' It should go away as fast as it came."

"Really?" He looked skeptical.

"Really," she repeated emphatically. "I'm undoubtedly allergic to something growing around here. There should be a killing frost soon. Then it'll be over."

"Suppose it isn't?"

"Then I'll go to the doctor and get a shot."

"We'll stop by the doctor today and you can get one."

"No, thanks."

"I'll pay for it," he said gruffly.

"That's very generous of you." She tried to ignore the feeling of guilt which swept over her at the false impression she was creating. Reporters had to stretch the truth occasionally to get a good story, she assured herself. It didn't help. She still felt guilty. "But I can't take medicine at the first sign of a sniffle. First, I'll try waiting for a killing frost."

"All right, but only for a few days. Now, tell me how sleeping on a straw mattress felt."

"Fine," she lied.

"Then we ought to switch beds," he said sourly, "because mine was scratchy, noisy and damned uncomfortable. So why wasn't yours?"

"I'm just the housekeeper here. I don't get to have an opinion."

"Wrong, you're the feminine viewpoint and how am I supposed to echo it in my book if all you ever say is 'fine and lovely?'" His voice was sharp.

"Tell you what, James, I'll make you a deal. You agree to keep me the whole two months and I'll give you the plain unvarnished truth."

"Are you trying to blackmail me?" His soft voice slid threateningly through her mind.

"Absolutely not! All I want is some job security."

"I told you I'd give you a kill fee." He glared at her in frustration.

"And I told you I don't take charity," Elspeth insisted, wondering if she'd pushed him too far. Claudia was right. He was not a safe man to cross.

"All right, you win," he said in exasperation. "You can stay the whole two months."

"Thank you, I—" She began to sneeze again.

"Come on." He grabbed her arm. "Let's go get breakfast. Maybe a good square meal will help."

"Can't hurt," Elspeth gasped, too happy with his concession to complain about having to trot to keep up with his long-legged stride.

Her glow of pleasure carried her through the twenty-minute trip into town and kept a smile on her face despite James's ordering her a breakfast which would have given a lumberjack pause. She simply ate the toast and drank the three cups of coffee she really wanted and ignored the rest.

"You don't eat enough." James frowned at her virtually untouched plate.

"It isn't that I don't eat enough. It's that you order too much." She glanced ruefully at the stack of pancakes, the mound of fluffy scrambled eggs, the strips of bacon and the pile of hash browns in front of her.

"Nonsense, I ordered us both the same thing, and I ate everything."

"I noticed. I'm beginning to think that equality between the sexes isn't all it's cracked up to be."

"It's a myth. Men may be stronger physically, but women are much deadlier."

"In what regard?" Elspeth was taken aback by his response to what had been a lighthearted comment on her part.

"Women take what they want and are perfectly willing to cheat to get it."

"Are you speaking generally or specifically?"

"I'm speaking too much. Now then, let's make our plans."

Despite her frustration at his change of subject, she made no attempt to return the conversation to his surprising statement. Thanks to his promise she now had a whole two months to collect information for her interview.

"What plans?" she asked.

"For what we're going to do today."

"Okay." Elspeth pulled a small pad and a pencil out of her purse and looked expectantly at him. "Go ahead. I'll take notes."

"We need to get food and pick up the supplies I've ordered."

"What kind of supplies?"

"Mostly equipment we'll need. Then I'll call and have the chickens delivered."

"Chickens?"

"Eighteen hens and a rooster. Colonial farms were virtually self-sufficient. They grew their own food, raised sheep for wool and tallow, grew flax for fiber and cut their own wood for heat."

"Busy little devils, weren't they?" Elspeth said hollowly.

"We won't be able to do all those things, not in two months," he said regretfully.

"Where did you find the old-fashioned equipment we need?" she asked curiously.

"It wasn't as hard as you might think. There's been a big revival in the folk arts which means that a lot of the old crafts are being rediscovered. Plus, New York State has a sizable population of Amish and their farming techniques haven't changed significantly since the 1600s, which means they have to manufacture the equipment they need."

"That makes sense. You say you've already ordered what we need?"

"Uh-huh. A couple of shops are holding things for me and I've had a lot of stuff sent to the Post Office care of general delivery. I'll pick it all up while you're getting the food."

James took his well-worn wallet out of his hip pocket and pulled out several bills, handing them to her. "I'll drop you off at the grocery store and come back for you when I'm finished."

Elspeth glanced down at the money she was holding, her eyes widening as she realized they were hundred-dollar bills. Whatever else James Murdoch might be, he wasn't stingy. She tucked the money into her purse and then said slowly, "I think before I buy groceries, I'd like to stop by the local library. Do you know where it is?"

"About six blocks from here. What do you want to go there for?"

"Ideas. The sum total of my knowledge of the Revolutionary War is that we won. I don't know what they ate or wore."

"What they wore is on a peg in your loft."

"Providing the movie company's information is accurate," Elspeth warned. "And even if it is, that still doesn't tell me anything about the types of food they ate."

"All right. We'll fit in a quick stop. You're sure you can't eat any more?" He reached for the bill.

"No, I'm through." She gathered up her purse and followed him toward the cash register at the front of the restaurant. Her eyes narrowed slightly as she watched the cashier give James the benefit of a wide, gleaming smile and a sultry look that was a clear invitation.

An invitation James ignored, Elspeth noted with a feeling of relief that made her vaguely uneasy. It was just because the cabin was so isolated, she told herself. If he were to develop an active social life, she'd be out there at night by herself.

James had no difficulty locating the library. He pulled into its well-paved parking lot, turned off the engine and then leaned back against the seat.

"Aren't you coming in?" Elspeth asked, when he made no move to get out of the truck.

"You don't need me to get your books."

"I don't need you, but it would be quicker if you combined your ideas with mine. I'm not sure exactly where to look for the information."

"You, with a college degree?" There was an edge to his voice that confused her. He sounded as if he had something against education, but that didn't make any sense. Not from a man who made his living writing books.

"This is totally unnecessary, Elspeth. I've ordered all kinds of books on the revolutionary period to be sent to me from a big bookstore in New York City. They should arrive sometime next week."

"That's then. This is now. Besides," she said with a laugh, "Saratoga Springs is so old they might have some original manuscripts from the period."

"All right. I surrender, but I'm only coming along to shut you up." The twinkle in his eye belied the harshness of his words.

"It's a good thing you didn't get your Valkyrie," Elspeth said tartly. "You're so irascible, she'd probably have mangled you the first day."

"The mind boggles at the thought."

"Not without a great deal of satisfaction."

Elspeth slipped through the wide library doors, then paused as something on the bulletin board caught her eye. "Just a minute, James."

She moved closer to read it.

"What is it?" He leaned over her shoulder and she tensed as the warmth of his body engulfed her.

Making a valiant effort to ignore the sensation, she pointed to the notice which had caught her attention. "This one about the farmers' market on Thursdays."

"So?" He shrugged and the movement sent a wave of his spicy after-shave over her receptive senses. "I told you. I've already ordered the livestock."

"You don't buy livestock at a farmers' market," she explained. "Haven't you ever lived in a small town?"

"Nope, except in Germany when I was in the service. I'm strictly a big-city lover."

Lover? The word unleashed a Pandora's box of images in her mind which had nothing to do with cities, big or otherwise. "I see." She cleared her throat. "Well, be that as it may, a farmers' market is a place where farmers bring their fresh produce to sell. It's exactly what we need."

"It is?" He looked unconvinced.

"Sure, because it's all local produce, so the colonists would have had it. At least in some form. We can stop on the way home. I'll ask the librarian where the west end parking lot is."

"Don't bother. I already know."

"Good." She paused in the middle of the lobby and glanced around, getting her bearings. "How about if we just try the card catalog this time and leave the pamphlets and magazines till another day."

"You can leave them permanently as far as I'm concerned," he muttered.

"Don't be a defeatist. What category do you think we should look under first? Colonial?" She turned to him. "You're undoubtedly a lot more knowledgeable about this than I am."

"I have never used a card catalog," he snapped irritably.

"You haven't?" She stared at him in disbelief. "But how do you get the necessary facts for your books? As I remember, one of them was built around the effects of a rather obscure poison. And another involved NATO policies."

"Interviews," he said. "I go see an authority and ask him questions and tape his answers. And, of course, the background was no problem since all my previous books were set in the everlasting present."

"Efficient," she conceded, "but it's hardly going to work now. You can't interview someone who's been dead for two hundred years." She pulled open a drawer in the card catalog.

"Oh, I don't know." He chuckled. "I remember once talking to a lady who was a whiz with a Ouija board."

"A whiz as an actress, more likely," Elspeth muttered. "Ah, here we go. Nine seventeen point three."

"What?"

"Nine seventeen point nine. You know. Dewey," she added at his blank look.

"Dewey who?"

"Not who, what. Dewey decimal. The library assigns numbers to books based on their subject. It makes it easy to find them."

"Maybe for someone with an education, but I told you I didn't go to college."

"I got news for you, friend. Education and college are not synonymous. Education isn't a body of knowledge. It's an attitude. A way of looking at life. And speaking of looking, we'd better get going. I want to get to the farmers' market before all the goodies are gone."

"Goodies?" He gave her an incredulous look.

"Goodies," she repeated firmly. "Just wait. You'll see." She headed toward the stacks. Her search was successful and she found a large selection of books on the colonial period. Hurriedly grabbing six likely-looking ones, she checked them out after first signing a declaration that she was a bona fide resident of the county.

"We do live in this county, don't we?" she asked James once they were back in the truck.

"Nope." He checked the traffic before pulling into the road.

"I figured you'd have said something if we weren't."

"You figured wrong. What difference does it make? We're not trying to steal the books."

"Yes, but if the rules say—"

"If you follow all the rules, you'll wind up knee-deep in red tape."

"Maybe." She gave him a doubtful glance, wondering just how far his avoidance of the rules extended. When you got right down to it, there was a surprising amount of the revolutionary spirit in James Murdoch. It could give an interesting slant to her article.

She opened one of her books and, flipping to the chapter on food, began to read.

"Well, do you know what you're going to buy?" James asked as he pulled up beside the entrance to a large grocery store.

"Yes, a big bottle of multivitamins," she said tartly. "From the sound of what they ate, it's a wonder they didn't all have beriberi and scurvy and pellagra and every other deficiency disease known to man."

"It takes years to develop those," he said. "We're only here for two short months."

Which seemed to be getting longer with every passing minute, she thought ruefully.

"Now what are you thinking?" He cupped her chin, turning her face toward him. The hard calluses on his palm felt rough against her soft skin, sending shivers of awareness through her.

Come on, Elspeth Fielding, she rallied herself. You're a thirty-three-year-old professional journalist and he's just your subject. Act like it.

"Your nose isn't red any more and the puffiness around your eyes has gone down," he observed with obvious satisfaction.

"Thanks. You've no idea what a comfort that is to me," she snapped, annoyed at his unflattering description.

"I imagine so." He released her chin, oblivious to her annoyance. A fact which only increased her irritation. Didn't he realize that a woman would take exception to being told her nose was red? Or, perhaps, he didn't think of his housekeeper as a woman, but merely as a pair of willing hands. Unexpectedly, the thought depressed her.

"Since I am recovered, I'd better get busy," she said. "If I get finished before you've run all your errands, I'll wait for you there." She pointed to the wooden benches in front of the store.

"I shouldn't be very long," he told her. "Although I think I will take advantage of having a phone available to call my publisher."

"There's no phone at the cabin," she said with a sudden realization.

"Of course not. Colonists—"

"—didn't have phones," she finished in resignation. "What they did have was an incredible accident rate. Maybe you ought to get a mobile phone for emergencies. I mean, it's not like either of us really knows what we're doing."

"I know exactly what I'm doing." James's features took on a haughty expression.

"If you say so." She gave in, not wanting to persist in the face of his obvious annoyance. It was quite clear that James did not appreciate aspersions being cast on his competence. And having a phone really shouldn't matter, she assured herself. What could happen in two short months? Hastily, she closed her mind to the myriad possibilities which immediately sprang to mind.

"See you later." She climbed out of the truck and headed into the store, determined not to keep him waiting.

However, as it turned out, he was the one who kept her waiting. Elspeth had been sitting on the bench in the warm sunshine reading for almost twenty minutes when she saw him pulling up.

"Get in. I'll take care of the sacks." James climbed out of the cab and began putting the two cartloads of groceries into the back of the truck.

"Thanks," Elspeth said thoughtfully. He didn't open doors or hold chairs for women, but he did their lifting. Interesting. She filed that bit of information away.

"Did you have any luck with your errands?" she asked when he'd finished.

"I had a bit of trouble contacting the man who sold me your chickens and cow, but I was finally able to reach him."

"My chickens and *your* cow and don't forget we're going to the farmers' market."

"I haven't, and the cow gives milk, which is a kitchen item so it should be your responsibility."

"Oh, no, it isn't." She began to leaf through the book she'd been reading. "You're the one with the fetish for accuracy and according to this, 'he'—that's the farmer— 'bred, milked, and pastured the cows.' "

"But I can't milk a cow!"

"I've never done whatever it is you do to chickens either, but am I complaining?"

"Yes," he said succinctly.

"Maybe a little," she conceded, "but I'm not trying to get out of it because I know how important accuracy is to you." She gave him a smug grin. "I think, my friend, that you have been hoist by your own petard."

"I think the cow is the one who's going to be in trouble. Here's your farmers' market." He pulled into the parking area. "Do you have any money left?"

"Of course I do! You gave me six one-hundred-dollar bills and I only spent two hundred and seventy-six dollars and forty cents at the grocery store."

"Ah, yes. Of course, a woman would know to the last dollar how much money she has." His voice held a sneer that infuriated her.

"I'm not a woman. I'm me, Elspeth Fielding, your hired housekeeper who is handling your money. And as long as I am, you'll get a receipt for every dollar and a written record of where every penny went. I won't be long," she snapped.

"Elspeth." His large hand on her shoulder stopped her as she started to get out. "I'm sorry. That was a nasty crack and you didn't deserve it. Even if most women do."

As an apology it left a lot to be desired. But this wasn't the time to try to strike a blow for womankind, she decided. For the moment, it was enough that he was willing to concede that she was different.

"Thank you. You want to come along and carry things?" She gestured toward the rows of stalls.

"Sure," he agreed, falling into step beside her. "And keep a couple of hundred dollars of the money I gave you as an advance against your salary."

"Thank you," Elspeth murmured, feeling guilty again.

Four

———

Here, hold this." James handed her a partially eaten apple. "I need both hands to negotiate our driveway."

"And the muscles of Charles Atlas," she added, as the truck bounced over the rough road.

"I finally tracked Wilder down. It seems his wife's been ill and he's gotten behind in his deliveries. He said he'll be able to bring a load of gravel out next Wednesday."

"Is a gravel driveway authentic?" She gave him a look of wide-eyed innocence. If she were going to have to suffer through the horrors of colonial housekeeping, he could put up with a rough road.

"Has to be. They've been mining stone in the Northeast for centuries."

"That's marble, and—" She gasped as he swerved around a huge chuckhole. "Be careful."

"You aren't going to turn out to be a back-seat driver, are you?" He frowned at her.

"Of course not. This truck doesn't have a back seat." She grinned at him.

"'A rose by any other name...'" he muttered.

"My God, the man quotes poetry!"

"I have quite a repertoire of quotations. Most of them would curl your ears."

"Go ahead," Elspeth dared him, "try. I think you'll find that modern women aren't quite as easily shocked as you seem to think."

"Maybe, but as you pointed out, you aren't women, you're you. And I don't think you're quite as sophisticated as you'd like to appear."

"I'm not the farmer's daughter, either."

"No, you're the farmer's housekeeper."

"Do you have any idea how annoying it is to have to put up with someone who always gets in the last word?"

"No, it's not a situation I often find myself in." He chuckled.

"Of course not, because..." She broke off as she caught sight of a man sitting on their porch. "Who's that?"

"*What's* that might be the more relevant question," James said dryly. "Although he could be the man with the livestock. I did all my business with him over the phone."

"Hmm." Elspeth studied the apparition. "You know who he looks like with those ripped overalls and that shaggy beard is Pa Kettle."

"Pa who?" James pulled the truck up in front of the small barn and cut the engine.

"Pa Kettle. You know, from the book *The Egg and I*. And a whole bunch of old movies."

"Never heard of him. Come on, let's find out what he wants."

"Maybe he's selling the local equivalent of white lightning. Maybe—" She broke off in horror as the old man suddenly spat an evil brown stream of liquid onto the barren ground beside the steps.

"James," she whispered, "keep him outside. If he were to forget and spit on my floor..."

"Squeamish stomachs were not a characteristic of colonial housekeepers."

"I wonder if hysterics were. Or, at least, an attack of the vapors."

"We throw water on hysterical outbursts." His voice was threaded with laughter.

"No doubt right after you shoot the horses."

"M'ster Murdoch?" The man heaved himself—all three hundred pounds—to his feet and held out a grubby hand.

Elspeth watched as James shook it, not seeming to notice its dirt-encrusted state. Her sources had been right. He wasn't a snob.

"Yes, I'm James Murdoch, and you are..."

"Silas," he boomed. "Just Silas. I brought the chickens you wanted."

Ha! Elspeth thought. That showed what he knew. As far as she was concerned, he could have waited till next year to deliver the wretched things.

"Real good layers, too, Miz Murdoch," he addressed Elspeth and she felt a warm flush tint her cheeks at the image his words brought to mind. Images of her and James sharing a bed. Images of their bodies pressed close together.

"It's Miss Fielding." James's clipped correction shattered the illusion.

"I'm the housekeeper." She forced a cheerful tone.

"Yes, ma'am," he mumbled. "Ain't no business of mine, I'm sure. Now, 'bout them chickens. I put them in that coop beside the barn."

"Coop?" she repeated.

"Course I was real careful to check for snakes first."

"Snakes?" she squeaked, instinctively moving closer to James's muscular body.

"Yup." Silas sent another stream of brown liquid to his left.

Elspeth kept her face expressionless with a monumental effort. Journalists have to be able to deal with all types of strange cultures, she told herself. She just wished this specimen wasn't on her own doorstep.

"It's a little late in the year for snakes," James comforted her.

"A little," Silas conceded, "but it always pays to keep your eyes open."

Especially around you, Elspeth thought, or who knows what one might step in.

"Now, I put the cow's hay in the loft and the chickens' feed in them bins in your barn. You didn't want the sacks, did you?" He peered hopefully at Elspeth.

"Oh, no," she replied, not having the vaguest idea what he was talking about.

"Good." He gave her a wide grin, displaying tobacco-stained teeth. "My old lady, she uses them."

"Speaking of the cow, where is it? In the barn?" James asked.

"Nah, this is Thursday."

Elspeth glanced at James's equally puzzled face and said, "I'll bite. What do we do with cows on Thursday?"

"Nothin'," he said as if astounded by such denseness. "That's why she ain't here."

"But the chickens are," Elspeth pointed out with an apprehensive glance at James. Rather to her surprise, instead of the angry impatience she'd expected, his expression was enthralled, as if he were fascinated by the old man.

"That's 'cause the chickens fit in the sidecar, and the cow, she don't," Silas said slowly, as if afraid that her intellect wasn't up to understanding his explanation.

"Sidecar?" Her eyes followed his gesture, suddenly seeing the motorcycle with his attached sidecar propped up against the end of the porch.

"How cute," she exclaimed.

"Cute!" Silas sounded outraged.

"Siegfried in 'Get Smart' had one of those."

"Ain't got no foreigners 'round here," Silas protested.

"No, on television," Elspeth explained.

"Ain't got much television, neither. Reception's bad unless you got one of them newfangled dishes. You see—"

"Yes, interesting as this may be," James's incisive voice cut in, "it still hasn't explained why the cow hasn't been delivered."

"Cause I need the truck to pull the trailer to bring the cow."

"It sounds just like a nursery rhyme." Elspeth was hard pressed to keep from giggling.

"My boy's got the truck. At the farmers' market," Silas added.

"I see." James nodded. "And when might we expect delivery on this cow, which I might point out I've already paid for?"

"Saturday," Silas promised. "Monday at the latest."

"Why not tomorrow?" James demanded.

"Possible, but it ain't likely. It being Friday and all."

"Fine," Elspeth broke in before James could say anything. She had no intention of standing here listening to another round of explanations. "We'll expect the cow when it comes and thank you for delivering the chickens. Now if you'll excuse me, I want to get the groceries unpacked."

"I'll help so's then the truck bed'll be free," Silas said.

"And why do we want the truck bed free?" James asked suspiciously. "We're not transporting that cow in my new pickup."

"Course not," Silas scoffed. "Your truck's sides ain't high enough. Fool beast'd tumble right out. I blew a tire when I hit a hole in that driveway of yours. And I figured the least you could do, being the good folks you are, was to give me a lift back home."

"And the most?" Elspeth asked.

"Well, them tires, they're right expensive. I don't know how I'm going to pay for a new one."

"With the profits from the exorbitant price you charged for the cow and the chickens?" James suggested.

"Exor..." Silas looked confused.

"Overpriced," Elspeth translated.

"Ain't overpriced," Silas protested. "Why, I raised them chickens myself right in my own kitchen."

"Kitchen!" Elspeth blinked. "They're not coming in my kitchen."

"Where they live is beside the point," James said in exasperation. "The point is—"

"That your driveway ruint my perfectly good tire," Silas repeated doggedly.

"Elspeth, give him fifty dollars."

"If you say so." She obediently dug a bill out of her purse and handed it to the old man even though she was of two minds about the wisdom of it. While she felt sorry that his tire was ruined, it had to have been in pretty poor shape to start with to have been punctured by simply running over a chuckhole. And she'd met Silas's type before. Chances were good that if he decided they were an easy touch, he'd be over here constantly trying to weasel things out of them.

"Thank you, ma'am." He hurriedly shoved the bill into his pocket as if afraid they might demand it back. "Well, now, M'ster Murdoch, let's get these things unpacked." He ambled toward the truck.

Elspeth turned to follow him, but James stopped her, his hand closing around her slender shoulder.

"You're a game little thing, but we'll do the lifting. You go decide where you want things put." He turned her around and gave her a gentle push toward the cabin. The strength of his fingers penetrated her thin sweater and imprinted themselves on her skin beneath it.

"Thanks," she murmured, hastily moving away so as to break the unsettling contact. What was it about James Murdoch? She worried the question around in her mind. Yesterday she'd attributed her uncharacteristic reaction to him to a combination of nervousness and fear that he wouldn't keep her. But today, he'd agreed to let her stay—so why was she still on edge? Try as she might, she couldn't come up with an answer. At least, not one that didn't make her sound like a sex-starved spinster, which she *knew* she wasn't.

Trying to ignore what she couldn't understand, Elspeth entered the cabin and cast a swift glance around. It looked exactly as it had when she'd left. Small, barren, cheerless and distinctly cold. Unconsciously, she straightened her shoulders. She'd give this oversize woodshed a homey feel if it killed her. And the way to start was with a little warmth. She eyed the huge ceiling-to-floor stone fireplace with a jaundiced eye. The chimney was probably full of birds' nests.

"Where do ya want this?" Silas staggered in under the weight of a bushel of apples.

"The pantry. Put everything in there." She gestured toward the open doorway to the left of the fireplace.

Elspeth frowned as it suddenly struck her that the pantry was hardly the place for the dairy products she'd bought and, since they had no electricity, they couldn't have a refrigerator. So what did that leave? An ice chest like picnickers used?

"What are you looking so worried about?" James spoke from the doorway.

"I was just wondering where to keep things cool."

"From the feel of this room, right here on the kitchen table."

"I'm serious."

"You think I'm not," he said wryly. "It's no wonder the colonists wore long wool clothes. They needed them to keep from freezing. Speaking of which, you have a springhouse, same as any colonial housekeeper. It's about ten feet from the back door," he threw over his shoulder as he entered the pantry.

"Does the springhouse have snakes, too?" she called after him.

"Naw." Silas emerged from the pantry. "A springhouse is too cold for snakes. They like warm places."

"Good." Elspeth started toward the door only to come to a precipitous halt at Silas's next words. "It's bats ya got ta watch out for in the springhouse."

"And that, Elspeth, is what is known as cold comfort." James's chuckle sounded heartless to her worried ears. Maybe she should follow up her interview of James with a series of articles on the horrors of colonial life. No, she rejected the idea. No one would ever believe her.

She found the springhouse exactly where James had said it would be. It was built of the same round fieldstones as the cabin's fireplace. Cautiously, she opened the rough wooden door and peered into the dank blackness. Telling herself not to be a coward, she boldly strode in, only to step in the middle of the coldest puddle she'd ever encountered.

"Damn!" Hastily, she hopped back, her teeth chattering.

"What's wrong?" James's voice startled her and she jumped forward, this time landing with both feet in the water.

"Nothing," she said tightly. "I simply discovered why they call it a springhouse." She squished as she stalked toward the house.

"You'd better change those shoes before you catch a cold."

"All right." She sprinted up the stairs to her attic, glad to have a few minutes to herself. Kicking off her wet loafers, she sank down onto the bed, grimacing as it rustled beneath her weight. Honestly, didn't those pioneers he was so keen on emulating have feather beds, too? Why couldn't he have used them instead of straw?

Absently, she rubbed her chilled feet. One thing was certain, that springhouse was as cold as any refrigerator. A giggle popped out as she remembered James's words. Cold comfort, indeed.

Pulling open the top drawer of her bureau to get a pair of socks, she paused as she caught sight of her notepad.

This would be a good time to jot down her initial impressions of James. Taking out her pen and paper, she sat down on the bed and tried to decide where to start.

At the beginning, she finally determined. When he'd met her at the airport. His casual apology for being late had been in keeping with his reputation for arrogance, but why he'd been late hadn't. Nothing she'd discovered in his background had led her to believe that he was a good Samaritan. And not only had he stopped to help at the scene of an accident, but he'd given Silas fifty dollars for a new tire. She added that information to her list. As a matter of fact he was extremely generous with his money, considering the amount he'd allotted to buy supplies and the advance he'd given her on her salary.

Of course, he had a lot of money. But, even so, it didn't necessarily follow that simply because he had it, he was willing to spend it. Especially on other people. She grimaced. Some of the wealthiest people she knew were also the stingiest. But James wasn't stingy. At least not with money. However, some of the cracks he'd made about women could hardly be called generous. She recorded his comment about women and money.

And what about his refusal to let her do any heavy lifting? Was that latent chivalry or simply common sense? After all, she wasn't very big, and, if she strained something, he would have to go to the trouble of finding himself a new housekeeper.

Which brought her to another point. She flipped the filled sheet over and began writing on the back. Why had he agreed to scrap his original idea of keeping her on a trial basis while Claudia looked for a replacement? Pity for her supposed poverty? Elspeth frowned, finding the idea completely unacceptable. She wasn't sure just what she wanted from James Murdoch, but pity wasn't it.

Perhaps—

"Elspeth?"

She jumped at the sound of James's shout from the bottom of the stairs and guiltily shoved her notebook under her pillow.

"What do you want?"

"To tell you that I'm running Silas and that contraption of his home. I'll be back in time for lunch."

"It'll be ready." She put as much confidence as she could into her voice. A confidence she was far from feeling. Lunch meant cooking and cooking meant a fire. She sighed, remembering her fears about the state of the chimney. Shoving her feet into her sneakers, she went down to check.

The chimney was in as bad a shape as she'd feared. It was so badly blocked with debris that she could barely see the blue sky when she poked her head into the monstrous fireplace and peered up.

Well, this is what he's paying you for, she told herself. Shifting through her library books on the kitchen table, she located a volume entitled *The Forgotten Arts*. A check of the index turned up an article on how to use and maintain a fireplace.

Sitting down on one of the battered oak chairs, she began to read. Ten minutes later, she had a clear idea of how to clean out a chimney. It appeared to be a simple enough operation. Messy, but simple.

All she needed was a heavy object, a cloth sack to put it in and some twine to use to lower it down the chimney. She glanced around the barren room, her eyes narrowing thoughtfully as she saw James's chest of drawers. A man's undershirt would make a bag if you tied up the sleeves. Of course, he might not like it because the shirt would be ruined, but on the other hand he had said he was hungry and what was one undershirt, anyway. She could pick him up a new one next time she went to town and he'd never know the difference.

Firmly squelching her doubts, she opened his drawer and extracted an undershirt. She took a second look around the room, but nothing looked promising for use as a weight.

Taking his undershirt with her, she went out to the barn to have a look around. Her luck was much better there. She not only found a length of thick logging chain to use as the heavy object and a mildewed length of clothesline to lower it into the chimney, but she also located an old wooden ladder with most of its rungs intact.

Gleefully, she dropped the chain in the shirt, tied the rope around it and lugged it and the ladder around to the back of the cabin, leaning it up against the storeroom's back wall.

From there, it was a simple matter to scramble up onto the roof. She was cautiously making her way toward the chimney when she heard the sound of the truck slowly maneuvering up the driveway.

She began to hurry. James would be wanting his lunch and she didn't even have a fire lit to cook it.

Bracing her slender body against the chimney, she carefully inserted the wrapped chain into it, gently swinging it from side to side as the book had recommended.

She paused as she caught sight of James crossing the yard toward the house. Fascinated, she watched as the sun frosted his black hair with glittering silver highlights. Her attention slipped lower, lingering on the way the muscles in his broad shoulders rippled as he adjusted the weight of the tray he was carrying. Tray? She yanked her mind away from its dreamy contemplation of his physical attributes and focused instead on what he was carrying. She squinted into the strong sunlight. They were red berries of some sort and there looked to be at least twenty quarts of the things. Now what could he want to do with that many berries? The answers that immediately came to mind were not very reassuring.

Ah, well. She turned back to her task. She'd worry about the berries once she'd fixed lunch. Slowly, she began to pull the chain up, hoping that she'd at least cleaned out enough to avoid a chimney fire. Although... She paused thoughtfully as she considered the ramifications of a fire. The roof would probably burn and they'd have to move out. No. Regretfully, she discarded the idea as unsporting. Besides, she concluded on a practical note, he'd probably write the fire into the book and she'd have to cope with no roof in addition to everything else.

She almost had the chain to the top when, suddenly, an enraged bellow echoed up through the chimney and she instinctively jerked backwards, almost slipping off her precarious perch.

"Elspeth! What the hell are you doing?"

Cautiously, she peered down the chimney, but it was impossible to see anything.

"Elspeth! Answer me!"

"Sorry, I thought that was a rhetorical question," she yelled back. "I mean, it should be obvious what I'm doing."

"What you're doing is giving me grounds for justifiable homicide! Get the hell down here before you break your neck."

"Honestly, men," she muttered, yanking on her chain. He'd probably gotten too close to the fireplace and some of the soot drifting down had soiled his clothes. She didn't know why he was so mad. She was the one who was going to have to figure out how to get them clean without benefit of a washing machine.

"Elspeth!"

"I'm coming." She hauled the chain out of the chimney and, after one rueful look at the incredibly filthy undershirt, decided this wasn't the time to take it down. If he got that upset over a little soot on his clothes, he'd probably come unglued at the sight of it.

Hastily, she wedged it between the chimney and the roof and scrambled down to the ladder, hoping she wasn't dislodging too many of the shingles.

Once on the ground, she resisted the impulse to stall for time by putting the ladder away. Squaring her shoulders, she marched around the house to face him.

"You certainly took your time getting down here!" he rapped out the second she entered the cabin.

She blinked, trying to see in the dim light. How should she play this scene, she wondered. Indignant that he was yelling? Penitent that she'd upset him? Maybe she ought to try simply playing dumb. The problem was, she wasn't sure which of those modes he'd best respond to. One thing was certain, she needed to calm him down. She'd try the time-honored soft answer, she decided.

"I was on the roof—"

"I know where you were!"

Lovely. She gritted her teeth, hanging on to her own temper with a real effort. "I had to come down slowly because roofs are dangerous and you don't want me to have an accident, do you?"

"Oh, no." His voice dripped sarcasm. "I wouldn't want you to have an accident. Never mind the ones you cause."

"Cause?" She frowned, stepping further into the room. "What are you babbling about? There was no one on the roof with me. I was—" She broke off as her eyes finally adjusted to the gloom and she got a good look at James. His head and shoulders were covered with a fine black powder. All except for the twin paths down his cheeks, washed clean by the rivulets of tears pouring out of his closed eyes.

Stark fear lanced through her, chilling her skin and tightening her abdominal muscles. "What happened?" she demanded.

"Well you might ask," he bit out.

"Cut the editorial comments and get to the facts. Did the soot land in your eyes?"

"Of course it landed in my eyes! I heard something in the fireplace and looked up the chimney to see what it was. The next thing I knew I was hit with..." He gestured toward his head. "Soot, creosote, leaves, twigs, and God only knows what else."

"Come on." She reached for his arm, caught sight of her filthy hands and glanced around the room in frustration. There was no place to wash and there wasn't time for her to draw water from the well. James needed help and he needed it now.

Rubbing her hands down over her already grubby jeans, she grabbed hold of his muscular forearm. The crisp hairs on it felt rough against her sensitive fingertips. Running her tongue over her suddenly dry lips, she made a valiant effort to suppress what she knew were totally inappropriate feelings.

"Will you come on?" She tugged on his arm, but it was like pulling on a tree. He didn't budge.

"In the first place, I don't want to go anywhere, and in the second, even if I did, I couldn't until these tears

clear up." He reached up to brush them away, and Elspeth hastily caught his hand.

"Don't do that. The tears are good. It's nature's way
of trying to wash your eyes out."

"You mean she had forewarning of you?"

"Can you open them, just for a minute?" She ignored his crack. Considering what she'd done to him, he
was entitled to a few.

"Why?"

"So I can assess the damage."

"You *are* the damage!"

"If it makes you feel better to assign the blame, then
by all means it was my fault. And now that we've settled
that, can we get on with trying to minimize the damage?
Open your eyes."

"All right, if it'll satisfy you." He managed to half
open them and Elspeth felt her stomach clutch in dismay. They were full of black soot.

"This is no time for a home remedy," she told him.
"You need an ophthalmologist. And don't give me any
bull about a colonist wouldn't have had access to a hospital because a colonist would have had enough sense not
to have stuck his head up the chimney in the first place!"
Her nonjudgmental tone slipped slightly.

"There is that," he muttered, "but I can't go anywhere when I'm crying."

"For heaven's sake, knock off the macho male bit and
use your head. We are talking about your eyes. You only
get one pair so you better take care of them."

"I will," he growled, "just as soon as the tearing
stops."

"Oh for—" Elspeth felt like screaming in frustration.
"You listen to me, James Murdoch. Either you get in that

truck or I'm going to drive to the nearest phone and call
an ambulance and let them deal with you.''

"You are a domineering..."

"We colonial types had to be. Now will you move!"

"You can't drive the pickup. It's a stick shift."

"Oh, yes, I can. I can also drive a school bus and an
eighteen wheeler."

"You, Elspeth Fielding, are turning out to be a surprise package and not all of it pleasant."

"People are like that. All people," she said significantly. "For example, who would have thought that you
had a streak of cowardice."

"Or that you would have been dumb enough to try to
use psychology to manipulate me." He was silent a moment as if considering the situation and then he said, "I'll
make you a deal. I'll go to the hospital with you if you
agree to get an allergy shot while we're there."

"But I don't—" she began in frustration.

"That's my offer. Take it or leave it."

"I'll take it," she said, capitulating. This was not the
time to argue.

"Here." He reached into his pocket and handed her
the keys to the pickup. "And you'd better not try to welsh
on our deal."

"I do not welsh on deals!"

"All women welsh on deals. It's in their genes." He
grimaced, and the realization of just how much pain he
must be in made her bite back her retort. First, she had
to repair the damage she'd done. Then she'd work on re-
forming his unreasonable attitude.

Five

———

"Now this one," the nurse behind the desk said, handing Elspeth a small orange tube, "is to put in his eyes at bedtime. And this one is for daytime use."

"Orange for night, silver for day. What happens if I get them mixed up?"

"Nothing. It's just that the nighttime medication has the consistency of axle grease, which rather blurs the vision. The other is clear."

"I see." Elspeth carefully put them in her purse. "When should he use them?"

"Whenever his eyes bother him."

"But he will be okay?" Elspeth asked for at least the tenth time since she'd delivered James to the emergency room over an hour ago.

"He'll be fine," the nurse said soothingly. "We've examined his eyes and all we found were a couple of very minor scratches on the left cornea. They're painful, but

they aren't the least bit dangerous. All things considered, he was very lucky."

"I'll say." Elspeth breathed a heartfelt sigh of relief.
"The whole thing was my fault."

"Don't be so quick to take the blame. Sticking his head
up the chimney wasn't one of the brightest moves I've
heard of," the nurse said dryly. "After all, he could have
gone outside and looked on the roof."

"Yes, he could have, couldn't he?" Elspeth said
slowly. Somehow, the fact that James was capable of bad
judgment made him seem more human, which in turn
made him infinitely more appealing. At least to her. But
would that make him more appealing to readers of her
interview? She frowned thoughtfully.

"Now, now." The elderly nurse patted Elspeth's
shoulder, misunderstanding her look of concern. "Quit
worrying. In a couple of days, he'll be back to his normal shape. Although the shape he's in right now sure isn't
bad." She chuckled. "If I'd have found someone like him
when I was your age, I wouldn't be single today."

"Oh, I didn't find him. He found me."

"Even better," the woman said approvingly. "You
take the word of one who's seen it all and let the men do
the chasing. Makes them feel like they're really in control."

"I wish someone was." Elspeth sighed, beginning to
feel distinctly frayed around the edges. One way and another, it had turned out to be a very trying day and it was
only half over. She glanced at the clock on the wall. It
was barely three.

"Now, you go sit down." The nurse pointed to a row
of grey plastic chairs against the wall. "He'll be out just
as soon as they finish washing his hair."

"What?" Elspeth stared blankly at her.

"Washing his hair," the woman repeated. "It's loaded with soot and bits of ash. The second he stands up, it'll fall in his eyes and we don't want to go through this again, do we?"

"Absolutely not," Elspeth said vehemently. "And thank you for your help." She walked over to the seats and sat down, leaning her head back against the wall. She closed her eyes, feeling tiredness drag at her limbs. All she wanted to do was to crawl into bed, even that straw monstrosity, and sleep for a week. But she couldn't. She still had to get the cabin organized, a fire lit, lunch prepared and then there was supper to worry about.

You can do it, she urged her flagging spirit. You're getting lots of great material for your interview. By the time this is over you'll have enough insights into his character to write a fantastic piece. Always provided you live so long. She rubbed her sore bicep where she'd received her allergy shot.

"Now watch your step, Mr. Murdoch. No! Keep your eyes closed. Just move a little to your left. Careful of the counter! Take baby steps."

Elspeth turned, watching as James was shepherded across the lobby by a young, blond nurse's aide. Elspeth frowned as his face darkened at the woman's irritating manner. Not that Elspeth blamed him. He might not be able to see, but that was no reason for the woman to treat him like a two-year-old.

Elspeth got to her feet, intent on rescuing him before his simmering temper reached flash point and consumed both the nurse's aide, who probably meant well, or herself, who definitely did.

"Thank you so much for your help, nurse," she said, hurrying over to them. "We appreciate it very much."

"All in a day's work. Although this is the first day we've ever had a famous author in here," she gushed.

"Famous author?" Elspeth repeated with a quick glance at James's taut features. His face was pale, and white lines radiated from the corners of his tightly compressed lips. His closed eyes were still tearing slightly, although with the soot gone from his face it wasn't quite as obvious as it had been.

"I recognized his name right away." The young woman nodded emphatically.

"Oh, you mean that author." Elspeth forced a grin when what she really wanted to do was to tell the woman to get lost. But that would be very shortsighted. She wouldn't put it past her to come to the cabin, and from James's reaction at the airport, she was sure he'd hate that. Nor did she herself relish the idea of fending off a persistent fan.

"Actually, they don't have exactly the same name," Elspeth confided in a stage whisper. "The real James Murdoch spells his name with an h and my Jim here spells his with a k."

"Oh. You mean he isn't a famous author?" She looked crestfallen.

"Sorry." Elspeth shrugged. "Although I bet you've met a lot of famous people in this town."

"Yeah. During the third week in August when the racing circuit's here." She gave James one last regretful look. "I should have known it wasn't true. Well, famous author or not, you take care of your eyes and follow Dr. Whitney's instructions, you hear?"

"Yes, ma'am." His voice was pregnant with suppressed feeling and Elspeth hurriedly grabbed his hand, anxious to remove him from the scene.

"Just hold my arm, James," Elspeth said. "We're about twenty-five feet from the emergency room entrance. We'll pass through a set of automatic doors and then it's about fifteen feet to the truck. There's no steps anywhere."

He fell into step beside her. "Thanks for heading off the autograph hound, although all she has to do is check the form you filled out to know that I spell my name with an h."

"It won't do her any good, even if she thinks of it." Elspeth chuckled. "By that time we'll be long gone. And the address won't help her. I didn't have the vaguest idea what the cabin's is, so I used my home address in Litton."

Elspeth heaved a sigh of relief as they passed through the automatic doors. "No one's towed away the truck. Here." She placed one of his hands on the door handle.

She waited until he was seated, then slammed the door closed. Hurriedly, she rounded the hood and climbed in. Inserting the key in the ignition, she glanced over at him, wincing as she noticed the fact that his complexion had gone from pale to light grey.

"Did they give you anything for the pain?" she asked. "I could go and ask for something."

"What you're asking for is—"

"I said I was sorry!"

"And that's supposed to make it better?" He partially opened his left eye and Elspeth winced at the sight of his red, inflamed orb.

"Nothing can make it better but time," she said tightly. "And that time is really going to drag if you persist in nursing a grudge."

"Please don't mention nurses." He leaned his head back against the seat.

Frustrated, Elspeth ground the gears as she backed the truck out of the No Parking zone. James Murdoch was in dire need of some lessons in how to handle interpersonal relationships. But this was hardly the time to give him one, she conceded. What he needed right now was a good meal and a nap. A long nap.

It would make a lot more sense to buy a sandwich to take back with them than for her to try to cook once they got there, she decided. Who knew how long it would take her to get a fire going and a meal prepared?

"How about if I pick up a couple of subs for lunch?" she suggested.

"I'm not hungry."

"I'm willing to fix you lunch back at the cabin," she offered. "I didn't want you to have to wait."

"Just get yourself a sandwich," he ordered.

"No thanks, but I'm not very hungry."

"I changed my mind," he said flatly. "I want a sub. Buy us each one."

"All right." Elspeth headed toward the business district, wondering if his about-face was simply a desire to be obstructive or if he really had changed his mind. She sighed. Maybe food would make him feel better.

It didn't. Not that he ate much, she thought, noting the way he played with his sandwich. And it was pretty good, too. She took another bite of hers. As a matter of fact, it was delicious.

"Would you like some of those raspberries you got from Silas, James? A few of them escaped the soot."

"No, this is fine. Go ahead and finish your sub."

"I've had all I want, thanks. Why don't you lie down?" she suggested, worried by the exhaustion threading his voice.

"I will just as soon as I've had a bath. There's soot and bits of ash in my shirt and pants and it itches."

"Oh?" Elspeth muttered, her eyes going to his flat stomach before slipping down over his snugly fitting denims to linger compulsively on the swell of his masculinity. She half closed her eyes as she pictured the tiny particles of black speckled across his pale skin.

"Okay?" James's voice shattered her thoughts. His tone was a clear indication that whatever he was asking, this wasn't the first time he'd asked it.

"I'm sorry." She forced her gaze upwards to his impatient face, glad he couldn't see well enough to notice her juvenile fascination with his anatomy. "What did you say?"

"I asked if you could fill the washtub in the pantry with water for me," he repeated.

"Of course. The water should be heated in half an hour." I hope, she thought, getting to her feet and peering at the fitfully burning fire she'd lit when she'd first come in.

"I don't want to wait. I'll just use cold."

"You're going to take a cold bath in here? You'll catch pneumonia to keep your scratched cornea company! This room is like an icebox."

"I'll survive. I survived primitive conditions in 'Nam."

"Yeah, but it was hot in Vietnam."

"It's going to get hot around here if you don't quit arguing with me."

"All right. It's your body." He was probably right, she reassured herself. A cold bath wouldn't hurt him. Surreptitiously, she crossed her fingers.

She hurried into the pantry, glancing in resignation at the haphazard way James and Silas had shoved her groceries onto the shelves. She'd straighten them later. First,

she had to get his bath ready. Looking around, she found
the washtub he mentioned.

She eyed it dubiously. Taking a bath in that thing was
not going to be easy. She stifled a giggle at the thought of
James trying to fold his muscular body into its two-foot
diameter. Don't laugh, she told herself. Your turn will
come. It was definitely a sobering thought.

Rummaging through one of the boxes on the floor, she
found round balls of what looked like homemade soap
and a stack of skimpy towels of a scratchy, linenlike material. It must be authentic, she thought. It was uncomfortable enough.

She carted the things back into the main room and set
them in front of the fireplace, hoping to give him the
benefit of any heat from the fire, which was beginning to
burn a little more brightly. Carefully, she added a slightly
bigger chunk of wood from the box to the right of the
fireplace, then picked up the two wooden buckets and
went to fill the tub.

Fifteen minutes later she emptied what seemed like the
hundredth bucket of water and heaved a sigh of relief.
Besides being icy cold, that stuff was heavy.

"Was it too much for you?" James asked worriedly.

"Of course not," she replied. "I'm simply not used to
lugging water. Very few western women are. I'll get used
to it," she said, hoping it was true. Her arms felt like
they'd been yanked out of their sockets.

"Well, scat while I take my bath before the water gets
cold," he said wryly. His hands went to the heavy silver
buckle on his belt.

Elspeth watched intently as his fingers began to unfas-
ten it. "That water can't get any colder without freezing." She dragged her eyes away from his hands'
seductive movement and forced her mind to more mun-

dane matters. "As a matter of fact, that's what I want to talk to you about."

"Freezing?"

Elspeth's concentration slipped as he pulled the belt out of his jeans and flung it in the general direction of the bed.

"No, water. Did you have that well tested?"

"Why? It's been in operation since the mid-1700s."

"Yeah, and people in the mid-1700s caught typhoid and dysentery and a whole host of equally nasty things from wells just like that."

"Don't you think you're being overly cautious?"

"Nope." She shook her head. "It's also an open well with a loose-fitting cover. All it takes is one of those squirrels scampering around it to squeeze underneath, fall in and drown. I don't need to tell you what a decomposing body would do to the bacteria count."

"You didn't need to tell me any of this. Now go away. I want to take my bath."

"All right, I'll be in the pantry if you need me." She abandoned the argument as he started to unzip his jeans.

Determinedly, she began to rearrange her supplies, trying to ignore the sounds coming from the main room. It proved impossible. Her mind insisted on providing images to go with the faint splashes she heard. Images of James's muscular body lightly covered with soapsuds. Soapsuds sliding down over rippling muscles to—

Her wayward thoughts were cut short by a thump, followed by a muffled curse. Fearing that he'd slipped and hurt himself, she rushed back, only to come to a precipitous halt at the sight of him half in and half out of the tub.

Embarrassment and other more elusive emotions rushed over her in waves. "Uh . . . sorry," she muttered, her eyes lingering on the pale skin of his flat hips. "I thought you fell."

"I wouldn't have far to go to hit the floor," he said dryly, "but as long as you're here, you might as well help." He sat back down in the tub.

"Help?" To her utter mortification, her voice cracked. What was it about this man that made her feel like an untried teenager instead of the mature woman she knew herself to be? If she could just capture in her interview even a hint of the masculine charisma he so effortlessly projected, it would be dynamite. The thought of her reason for being here in the first place helped her to regain some semblance of her normal confidence.

"The ball of soap slipped out of my hand and rolled somewhere. And I can't see well enough to locate it. Would you find it and then get me two more buckets from the well?"

"You don't need more water." She came closer, frowning as she saw the bluish tinge of his lips. "What you need is to get out of the water you've already got."

"I will, just as soon as you get me some water to rinse with. This homemade soap leaves a scum. Just look at it." He gestured toward his chest and obediently Elspeth looked, her eyes following the thick cloud of jet-black hair which arrowed down to disappear into the dingy grey water.

"You see?" he said in disgust.

A whole lot more than is good for my peace of mind, she thought ruefully. "What I'm beginning to see is why the colonists emulated Queen Elizabeth."

"Queen Elizabeth?" He frowned. "What's she got to do with anything? She's only been around since the thirties."

"Not that one, the first Queen Elizabeth. She used to take a bath twice a year whether she needed it or not. And, if she had to put up with conditions like this, I'm surprised she did it that often. I'll be right back." She picked up the bucket. "Don't go away."

"Don't go away!" he repeated incredulously. "Where the hell would I go, naked, freezing, and blind?"

"Don't ask me," she threw over her shoulder. "You're the one with the imagination."

"Somehow I never imagined *you.*" His quiet words seemed to echo through her mind, filling her with a sense of uncertainty. What had he meant? she wondered as she drew two buckets of water from the well, shivering slightly as the icy water sloshed over the bucket rim to dampen her jeans and trickle down into her sneakers. Probably nothing, she finally decided. In fact, all things considered, it's a wonder the poor man wasn't raving by this time.

"Here you are." Elspeth set the full buckets beside the tin washtub. The faintly whooshing sound the water made when he stood up unnerved her, and with a hastily muttered, "I'll be in the pantry," she beat a quick retreat to the sound of James's amused chuckle.

Blasted man! He knew he was embarrassing her. Although considering the type of women he normally associated with, he'd probably been expecting her to try to climb in with him. At least, that had been the type of woman he'd associated with early in his career.

Thoughtfully, she went back to bringing order out of the chaos in her pantry. Despite her intensive research she hadn't been able to come up with the name of a single woman he'd been associated with since he'd suddenly left California and moved to New York eight years ago. As far as she'd been able to discover, his present life-style was almost monastic. There were no parties, wild or otherwise, no conspicuous consumption and no flagrant flouting of society's rules. It was almost as if he were a split personality.

The California years had shown a hard-drinking, hard-living hedonist who'd been well on his way to forging a formidable reputation for the pursuit of pleasure in a town where self-gratification was considered the norm.

Elspeth shifted a sack of cornmeal onto the second shelf as she considered the puzzle. There had to be a key, but what? Could it be the starlet he'd been living with? Could there have been some truth in those articles she'd read about how the woman's marrying someone else had devastated his life?

Having met James, she simply didn't believe it. He radiated too much inner strength and force of character to ever go into a decline because some woman had rejected him. Especially a decline that had lasted for eight years.

Besides, she reminded herself, to buy that theory you also had to believe that he'd been rejected by the woman he loved. A vision of James's bright blue eyes glittering with emotion and his firm lips curved in a sensual smile filled her mind.

She could almost feel the hard contours of his body. A tingling sensation danced over her breasts, and they tightened painfully. She took a deep breath, trying to dispel the sensation, but the heated air in her lungs only seemed to make her more aware of her own body.

"Elspeth!" James's impatient bellow shattered her daydream and brought a rueful smile to her lips. And then again, maybe it wasn't so hard to believe that his ladylove had tossed him aside. Sexy he might be, but romantic he most definitely wasn't.

"Coming." She set down a bag of dried beans and went back into the main room to find James dressed in a pair of faded jeans. He was standing in front of the closed back door, holding the washtub filled with his bathwater. "What are you doing?" she demanded.

"Emptying the bath water. Open the door."

"I can empty it."

"Don't be ridiculous," he said testily. "You had enough trouble carrying it a bucket at a time. Now quit arguing and open the door."

Elspeth did, worried about the pain which seemed to be muffling his voice. Arguing with him would only prolong things, not change them. Short though her acquaintance with him was, she was beginning to realize that he could be incredibly stubborn.

A feeling of tenderness, heavily spiced with guilt, welled up in her as she watched him cautiously make his way off the porch, pausing every couple of feet to force open his eyes so that he could see where he was going.

With snail-like persistence, he inched his way down the slope past the outhouse before upending the tub onto the hard ground. Then, to her horror, he swayed slightly and the tub slipped out of his hands, landing on the ground with a resonant thump.

That did it, she thought. He needed help and he was going to accept it, masculine pride or not. She sprinted down the slope. "Here. Lean on me." Elspeth put her arm around his waist, her fingers digging into his bare flesh just above the waistband of his jeans.

To her relief, James made no attempt to brush her off. Instead, he draped his arm over her slender shoulder, his hand dangling loosely over her right breast.

Oh, boy. Elspeth took a deep breath as his fingers brushed against her nipple and it hardened with desire.

The faint spiciness of the soap he'd used had been warmed by his body to an intoxicating aroma which filled her nostrils and drifted down into her lungs. Trying to ignore the coiling sensation in her abdomen, Elspeth urged him toward the cabin.

"Here we are," she said with a brightness that rang false even in her own ears. Opening the door, she helped him across the room, breathing a sigh of relief when he was finally stretched out on his bed. She resisted the impulse to spread a blanket over him. He might have allowed her to help him, but somehow she instinctively knew that James Murdoch was not a man who would appreciate being fussed over.

"Can I get you anything?" Her eyes played down over his lean length stretched out on the mattress.

"How's the fire going?" he asked.

"Fire?" She turned and looked. "Great, as a matter of fact. Why?"

"Do you suppose you could make me a cup of strong coffee?"

"Well, unfortunately, if you'll remember, I read the section on colonial cooking from that library book on the way to the grocery store."

"What does that have to do with my drinking coffee?"

"It has to do with your stated desire for authenticity. According to what I read, coffee wasn't much used by the colonists until the Revolution started and tea became so hard to get. And since your book starts out in the early 1770s..."

"You bought tea instead," he said in resignation.

"I could go get some coffee for you," she offered. "It wouldn't take me long."

"No." He flung his arm over his eyes. "We'll start as we mean to go on. Brew the tea. Just make it strong."

"I'll have it ready in five minutes," she promised.

It took her slightly longer than five minutes to solve the problem of how the black iron teakettle fit on the crane which was embedded on the back of the fireplace, and exactly how high the fire had to be before the water would boil. But once she figured that out, the rest was easy and it was with a distinct feeling of triumph that she carried a steaming cup of tea to James.

"Here you are." She carefully placed it in his hands. "Be careful, it's hot."

"Hm, it smells good." He sniffed the rising steam and then took a sip. "And it tastes even better." He took a second sip. "As a matter of fact, it tastes delicious. I don't remember tea being this good."

"Thank you." She felt a warm glow at his praise. "But a lot of the credit has to go to the Glenlivet I put in it. I figured you could use a good stiff dose of Scotch to take the edge off things."

"I knew this tea was too good to be true." He shifted his legs slightly. "Sit down a minute and have some with me. After the day you've had you could use a rest."

Taking his words at face value, she poured herself a cup and then gingerly sat down beside him. He was right. The mixture was good. It slid down her throat, warming her stomach even as his thigh was pressing into her back, warming her skin. She relaxed and allowed herself to enjoy it.

Six

That should do it." Elspeth's critical gaze swept around the small cabin. Everything was in order for her to fully assume her role of colonial housewife tomorrow. All she had left to do was to read the section in one of her library books on dealing with the intricacies of cooking over an open fire. And she really should record James's reaction to his accident while it was still fresh in her mind.

Thoughtfully, her gaze swung to the corner of the cabin where he was sprawled on his bed. He'd fallen asleep shortly after she'd dosed him with the tea and whiskey and he'd stayed asleep, seemingly oblivious to the sound of her working.

Picking up the tin candle holder with its flickering tallow candle, she crept closer. Stopping a few feet from him, she held the light above her head in an attempt to get a better look at his face. Unfortunately, it was turned away from her, so she couldn't check his eyes to see if the swelling and redness were going down and she was reluctant to move closer for fear of waking him. To say nothing of scalding him. She hurriedly shifted the candle holder to her other hand as the hot tallow dripped on her. *Maybe James has the right idea.* She stuck her scorched finger in her mouth. *Maybe it was time to go to bed.* Fascinated, she watched the steady rise and fall of his chest. God knew she was tired enough, even if it was only 9:30.

Briefly, she weighed what she should be doing against the dubious comforts of her straw mattress. She'd compromise, she decided. She'd go to bed and work on her interview there. But first she intended to have a bath. She was hot, tired, and dirty. And even the thought of that antiquated tin washtub of his seemed appealing. Although not with cold water. She glanced in satisfaction at the steam rising from the huge black kettle suspended from the fireplace crane over the roaring fire. Colonial living wasn't totally impossible, it just required a lot of foresight.

Her first thought was to have her bath in the relative privacy of the pantry, but the icy air which attacked her the second she left the main room gave her pause. Even with hot water, she could get pneumonia bathing out here. But what choice did she have, she thought, considering her options. Her loft? There was no way she would be able to lug enough water upstairs and it was probably cold, too. The only source of heat in this whole benighted cabin was the open fire.

She stuck her head back into the main room, peering uncertainly at the large blanket-covered lump that was James. She could hardly wake him up and ask him to go upstairs for a while. But maybe it wouldn't be necessary. After all, he'd been sound asleep for hours, despite all her activity. It would be a reasonable assumption that he'd stay asleep while she took a quick bath in front of the fire. She gazed longingly at the crackling blaze. She could put the two kitchen chairs between the tub and the bed and drape a blanket over them to create a screen.

A wayward puff of chill air slithered across her ankles, deciding her. She'd do it. As long as she was quiet, she shouldn't have any trouble. She didn't. Her screen went up with remarkable efficiency. Of course, it was only three feet high, which meant that she had to scrunch down like a pretzel to get undressed, but that was better than freezing.

A blissful sigh escaped her lips as she folded her aching limbs into the six inches of hot water in the bottom of the tub. For a few minutes, she simply relaxed in the warm glow of the fire before she picked up one of the little balls of homemade soap.

She was happily lathering her thighs when the rustling sound of James rolling over made her freeze. Nervously, her gaze swung toward him and a dismayed gasp escaped her as she realized that her screen was falling apart. The blanket had slid off one chair, giving her a clear view of the bed, and, more importantly, giving James a clear view of her.

If he were awake, she reminded herself. And there was no reason to assume he was, simply because he'd turned over. Cautiously, she crept out of the tub and tiptoed, dripping wet, to replace the screen before scurrying back to her bath.

Although she could probably have left it down, she assured herself. If James had woken up and seen her, he'd undoubtedly have said something. He was not the least bit reticent, she thought ruefully.

She rinsed herself and reached for her towel from the floor beside her. Even with the heat of the fire, there was no inducement to linger in her cramped bath. And, anyway, she needed to get upstairs and work on her interview.

But when she climbed between the rough sheets and propped her notebook on her lap, she found it very difficult to concentrate on James Murdoch the writer. Her mind kept straying to James Murdoch the man, to his physical presence and the intricacies of his personality. A personality she found fascinating. Altogether too fascinating. She grimaced. She was finding it almost impossible to maintain a professional detachment where James Murdoch was concerned. Her own reactions kept getting in the way.

Finally, she tossed the notebook onto the bedside table in disgust and blew out the flickering candle. She'd work on the interview in the morning. Right now, she was simply too tired to concentrate.

But tired as she was, she tossed and turned on the lumpy straw mattress for what seemed like hours. Finally, toward midnight she drifted into an uneasy sleep only to be awakened a few hours later by a heavy thump. Startled, she sat up, looking around her moonlit loft in confusion.

The cabin. Her memory rushed back. She was at the cabin and that noise from downstairs had to have been caused by James. Had he gotten out of bed and tripped over something? With his limited vision, it was a distinct possibility. Hastily, she flung back her covers and, grabbing her cold candle stub, rushed downstairs.

She found James sitting on the edge of the bed, his body clearly delineated by the bright moonlight streaming in through the bare windows. His head was in his hands and his shoulders were slumped as if in defeat. His vulnerable pose tore at her heart, filling her with a confused mixture of guilt, tenderness and concern. She bit back her impulsive words of sympathy, almost certain they'd be rejected. Instead, she calmly lit her candle stub and set it on the table.

"Are your eyes bothering you?"

"That isn't quite the way I would have put it, but that's the general idea. I'm sorry I woke you," he growled. "You need your sleep."

"No problem."

She carefully arranged several pieces of wood over the glowing embers in the fireplace, then washed her hands in the water left from her bath.

"I have something for your eyes," she said.

"Not one of those remedies from your books?" he asked suspiciously.

"No, this is a remedy from the hospital. An ointment." She dug it out of her purse.

"I don't want it."

"Lean your head back and open your eyes." She ignored his less than enthusiastic response.

"I said—"

"There's no reason to be afraid. I'm not going to hurt you."

"I am not afraid! And I told you not to practice psychology on me."

"What I'm going to practice on you is my judo! Now sit still." She knelt on the bed beside him.

"Damn it, woman! You have the persistence of a gnat."

"Talk about the pot calling the kettle black." She gently pushed back his left eyelid, wincing at the sight of his reddened eye. "I think it looks a little better," she lied.

"And I think you've been drinking the Glenlivet straight." He jerked as she squeezed out a thin stream of the ointment.

"Hold still." She put some in the other eye and then capped the tube and climbed off the bed.

"Where are you going?"

Elspeth paused at the plaintive sound of his voice. He sounded almost lonely. "Just to put your medicine away. To show there's no hard feeling I'll let you have some of my Scotch."

"Just what I need. A housekeeper with her own private stash."

"At least I'm willing to share." She poured him a generous amount in a china mug.

"What else are you willing to share, Elspeth Fielding?" His fingers brushed against hers as he carefully took the cup.

Elspeth felt the touch of his warm fingers like the unexpected jab of a pin. She curled her hand into a fist to dispel the inexplicable feeling. What was the matter with her? she demanded of her wayward senses. Why should this man's touch affect her so? He was only her employer. But her employer in a rather bizarre set of circumstances. She shot a quick glance at James, who was slowly sipping the potent drink. His black hair was tousled from sleep and a strand had tumbled enticingly down over his forehead. There was a heavy shadow along his jawline from his emerging beard and she shivered as she imaged the raspy feel of it against her own smooth cheek. Face it, she told herself. He might be your employer and the subject of your interview, but he's also a very sexy man.

But it was more complex than that, she realized. She'd spent the week before she'd joined him digging up every fact about him she could find. As a result, she knew more about James Murdoch than she did about people she'd known all her life. That knowledge had combined with an instant physical attraction and her liking of him as a person to make it almost impossible to keep him in perspective. And that would have to stop. Her interview had to be unbiased, she reminded herself. That was one of the basic tenets of good journalism.

"Apparently, you don't even share speech." He took her arm and, with a gentle tug, pulled her down beside him. "Sit down."

"I really should go back to bed," she said halfheartedly, trying to block out the pervasive warmth coming from his thigh, which was only inches from hers.

"Don't go yet. It's so dark and I can't see," he muttered, as if the admission were forced out of him. "You make it seem a little lighter."

"That's just my candle." She masked the sense of warmth which swept over her at his words.

"No," he said slowly. "It's you. I've never met a woman quite like you before. You have the kind of integrity that shines out."

Elspeth winced, almost feeling herself shrinking under the weight of the guilt and shame which filled her. The well-deserved weight, she admitted. It wasn't integrity he saw shining in her eyes. It was greed for what an interview with him could do for her. It could help him, too, she told herself, but, somehow, the reminder—true as it was—did nothing to make her feel better.

"Here, let me have that." She took his empty mug and set it on the floor. "Now lie back down."

"But I'm not sleepy and I don't want you to go."

"I'm not going anywhere just yet and, if you're not sleepy, why don't you tell me something about your book."

"Such as?" He leaned back and, picking up her hand, threaded his hard fingers through hers. It gave her a curiously protected feeling, as though as long as she held onto his hand she was safe. You're nuts, she warned herself. Security comes from within, not from another person. And even if it did, James's past record with women didn't make him a prime candidate for any lasting relationship. Although it did make him great copy. And the more information she could get, the greater the copy would be, she reminded herself.

"Such as why you're suddenly abandoning thrillers when they've made you so famous. To say nothing of wealthy."

"I haven't abandoned the thrillers. I simply don't want to write them exclusively."

"Run out of ideas?" She tried to sound sympathetic.

"No, inclination."

"But why a revolutionary saga?" she persisted.

"Why are you so interested?" His voice sharpened and Elspeth hastily backed off.

"Because I'm so involved. Just think, if you'd have had the foresight to do a novel set in prerevolutionary France, maybe I could have been Marie Antoinette and, instead of struggling with housekeeping, I could have sat around eating sweetmeats all day."

"Too much leisure stifles the mind and erodes the spirit."

"Well, if the opposite is true I ought to be bursting with spirit," she said tartly.

"To say nothing of impudence." He chuckled.

"So tell me about your book." She swallowed a yawn.

"Well, the main character is a middle-class farmer, named Abel Fletcher, who's determined to better himself at any cost."

"Oh?" Elspeth said hollowly as his words jabbed her already guilty conscience.

"It's the old Greek concept of taking what you want, but being prepared to pay for it."

"Yeah, but from what I've noticed when people start taking what they want, it's usually the people around them who pay the price."

"To some extent." His face momentarily hardened and Elspeth wondered what unpleasant memory her words had triggered.

"So how does this farmer of yours better himself?" She tried to pull him back to the present.

"He starts out by marrying the only daughter of the town's leading citizen, who's fallen on hard times."

"And he comes to love her?"

"No, he already loves Mary Fox, the indentured girl, who works at his parents' farm. As a matter of fact, he gets her pregnant and it's their son who brings about Abel's downfall."

"From the sound of things you should have called him Cain! You know, James, your hero sounds like a twerp."

"No, simply a man with a good and a bad side. He does have some heroic qualities, but the force that drives him is ambition and that ambition not only brings him what he wants, but also sows the seeds of his eventual destruction."

"Hm," Elspeth murmured, not liking the sound of his words. They were a little too close to home for comfort. "Tell me about the servant girl." She tried to steer the conversation in a new direction.

"All right." He began a rambling monologue. Finally, after almost fifteen minutes, his deep voice stopped as he drifted off to sleep.

Wiggling the stiff muscles in her shoulders, Elspeth tried to slip off the bed, but his fingers tightened convulsively around hers and he shifted restlessly. Elspeth frowned. If she yanked her hand free, she'd probably wake him up and his sleep had been disturbed enough as it was. She decided to wait a little longer to go back to her own loft. Just until his sleep deepened and his grip relaxed somewhat. But she was going to wait in relative comfort. She stretched out on the narrow strip of mattress between James and the edge of the bed.

Despite her intention of staying awake, her eyelids slowly slid shut and she sank into the deep, dreamless slumber of total exhaustion.

It was the cold that finally woke her. A deep, penetrating cold that had turned her slender body, clad only in a thin flannel nightgown, into a shivering icicle.

Reluctantly, she lifted her eyelids, frowning as she felt them brush against something. Something warm.

Groggily, she tried to focus in the moonlight. James. Her eyes widened in horror. The warmth she'd been trying to get closer to was James's body. She propped herself up on one elbow, causing the mattress to rustle.

Elspeth watched in dismay as James muttered protestingly in his sleep, then reached out to pull her back down against him.

"Go back to sleep, woman," he muttered.

Elspeth froze, not daring to move a muscle until his breathing had resumed its even cadence.

Who had James thought she was when he'd called her "woman"? She worried the question around in her mind. Was he romantically involved with someone despite the fact that she hadn't been able to find any evidence of it? Or had her presence beside him in bed merely triggered old memories? God knew he had enough of them to call on. Accounts of his days on the West Coast read like a playboy's dream.

One thing was certain: James hadn't realized it was she. A feeling of relief washed through her. Life in this tiny cabin would become unbearable if he thought she was trying to insinuate herself into his bed. She grimaced at her own stupidity. She should never have ventured out of her loft in the first place, thump or no thump. But failing that, the next best thing would be to get herself back upstairs before he woke up and found her snuggled up next to him. Cautiously, she tried to inch toward the edge of the bed, but his arm merely tightened.

Now what? She beat her exhausted mind for a solution, but nothing surfaced beyond the fact that the heat of his body was slowly warming her frozen limbs.

She tensed as she felt a sneeze building up. Oh, no! She clenched her teeth and her body shook convulsively with the imploded sound.

"Poor baby," James murmured. He slipped his arm beneath her shoulder and turned her tense body into his.

Elspeth swallowed uneasily as he began, slowly, sleepily, to nuzzle her neck. The overnight growth of his heavy beard rasped over her skin, sending a cascade of sensation flowing through her. Elspeth gritted her teeth, fatalistically waiting for him to wake up. To her amazement, he didn't. Apparently James was experienced enough to make love in his sleep, she thought, biting her lip against a hysterical urge to laugh.

A gasp escaped her as his free hand slowly moved up over her rib cage. Elspeth held her breath waiting for it to reach its destination. She didn't have the slightest doubt it would. Awake or asleep, James Murdoch had fantastic reflexes.

As if in concert with his marauding fingers, his lips, expanding their field of exploration, moved up over her chin and along her jawline toward her ear.

Tiny sparks of heat darted through her body to collect in a heavy coil of desire in her abdomen.

She had to escape. Now. Before he woke up entirely. Or before she became so engrossed in his kiss that she no longer cared if he did or not, as long as he didn't stop. And that point was perilously near, she admitted honestly. She didn't know what James Murdoch had, but whatever it was, she was highly susceptible to it.

But her tentative retreat was cut off as his lips closed over hers with unerring accuracy. At the same instant, his hand finally cupped her small breast through the thin material of her nightgown.

Her choked cry of pleasure was swallowed up in the warm cavern of his mouth. Aggressively shaping her mouth to his, his tongue surged inside, then penetrated deeper as if he couldn't get enough of her. A hot, melting sensation flowed through her, dissolving her initial resistance.

It had been so long since she'd been kissed with such driving masculine need, and she found that need almost as overwhelming as her own response. Mindlessly, she pressed closer to his warm, callused palm, which was slowly rubbing back and forth across the sensitized tip of her breast. It hardened under the delectable friction and she shuddered with a combination of pleasure and growing desire. The air in her lungs seemed charged with static electricity, sending sparkles of silvery excitement through her bloodstream.

Daringly, she touched the tip of her tongue to his and his fingers closed with almost painful force over her breast. It was a pain that was so mixed up in the pleasure she was feeling that she barely noticed it in her growing compulsion to delve deeper into the delights he was offering. But to her intense disappointment, his kiss stopped almost as suddenly as it had begun. With a sleepy mutter that she couldn't understand, he rolled over, freeing her.

For a brief second, Elspeth simply lay there, too shaken by both his kiss and her reaction to it, to do anything. Then, her sense of self-preservation surfaced through her rioting emotions and she hastily scooted off the bed and beat a hasty retreat to her loft.

And it was a retreat, she admitted honestly. Her brief sensual encounter with James had left her shaken and confused. Confused both about herself and about him. She needed time to come to grips with her feelings. But, at least James himself wasn't aware of what had happened. Since he had never woken up, she wasn't going to have to face a knowing gleam in his eyes the next morning. The thought consoled her somewhat.

One thing was certain, though, she decided as she wiggled restlessly, trying to find a comfortable position in her lumpy mattress. She was definitely going to have to put their relationship back on a more professional basis. Or, more precisely, establish it on a professional basis. So far there'd been nothing even vaguely orthodox about their working together.

Seven

Umph." Elspeth buried her head under her thin pillow, trying to escape the raucous sound of a cawing crow right outside her window. It was impossible. The grating noise followed her, flooding her ears and drowning her sleep.

Giving up, she levered herself up on her elbow and reached for her wristwatch which was lying on the bedside table. 5:40? "Five-forty!" she muttered in disbelief. That blasted bird had gotten her up at 5:40 in the morning! Those nursery rhyme people had sure had the right idea when they'd put blackbirds in pies. If she got her hands on that feathered sadist... Suddenly she remembered another kind of fowl—chickens. Her chickens. What kind of hours did chickens keep? she wondered. Would they be hungry at this time of the morning or should she feed them later?

Considering her track record for accidents, she might not be alive to do it later, she thought pessimistically.

Besides, if she fed and watered the things now, she'd have it out of the way.

She flung back the covers, shivering as the icy air pounced on her body, sucking away the heat. "Oh, what I wouldn't give for a quartz heater and an outlet to plug it into," she grumbled as she climbed out of bed. It was only two months, she encouraged herself. Two short months and she'd have her interview. Her eyes swung to the top drawer where her notes were hidden. She could take the time now to jot down James's reaction to the accident before she started her day's routine. \

And are you also going to jot down your reaction to him? she asked herself. I can see the headline now. Thirty-three-year-old would-be journalist throws herself at famous author. She winced as the memory of his kiss flooded her mind.

Sinking back down on the bed, she tucked her freezing toes under her as she tried to rationally assess what had happened. It was hopeless. Nothing about that kiss had been rational. Not its setting, and most emphatically not her headlong response. Somehow, the minute he'd touched her, her mind had cut out and her emotions had taken over. There'd been no thought involved, no conscious decision to kiss him. It had been instinctive, like a plant turning to the sun. Her body had recognized something in James, something that had caused it to flower in a way it never had before. It made no sense. She sighed in frustration.

James might be a highly complex person with intriguing depths that she hadn't expected to find, but in no way did he resemble the hazy image in the back of her mind of the man she someday hoped to meet. That man was a cross between David Niven, with his sophistication and Cary Grant, with his debonair manner.

She closed her eyes, trying to bring her long-held image into focus, but she couldn't. It kept wavering beneath the reality of James's roughly hewn features.

Don't you dare fall in love with him, she warned herself. You're here to get an interview. An interview to set up your future. She was only too aware of the fact that falling in love with James Murdoch would do lots of things to her future—none of them good. She didn't even need her extensive research to convince herself that loving James was a horrendous idea. One look at him was sufficient for that. The man positively oozed untrammeled masculinity. Not even her imagination was sufficient to picture him tying himself down with a wife and kids.

Not that she wanted him to. She had her own plans. Her eyes strayed back to the drawer with her notes. She was going to be a journalist, she reminded herself. A topflight journalist. But, somehow, her enthusiasm had dimmed over the past few days. And no wonder, she told herself, trying to bolster her spirits. A stint in the 1770s would be enough to take the icing off anyone's gingerbread.

Resolutely, she got to her feet. She'd save working on her interview as a treat for this afternoon. Right now, she'd get busy on what had to be done. And speaking of what had to be done... She eyed the period costume hanging on the peg beside the bed. At least it would be warm. And scratchy, she realized in dismay as she picked the dress up and the rough texture of the heavy fabric grated over her skin. Considering the uncomfortable clothes they had to wear, it was no wonder the era had had so many hotheads, she thought ruefully.

She looked back at the wall, noticing for the first time the rest of the costume. She only gave a cursory glance to the apron. It was the undergarments that held her attention. There was a voluminous slip consisting of yards of skirt which fastened with a drawstring around the waist, as well as a one-piece linen chemise, which laced up at the bodice.

Elspeth stared at the chemise in disbelief. There was no way she was going to wear that, and besides, James wouldn't know. He could hardly ask to check her underwear. A slow flush warmed her chilled body at the thought.

Crunching the slip and chemise into a ball, she shoved them into her bottom drawer and hurriedly slipped on the oversize dress. She crept down the stairs, pausing at the bottom to peer across the room at James. All that was visible was a long lump under the covers and a shock of dark hair against the coarse yellow-white linen pillowcase. Deciding that the longer he slept, the longer it would be before he demanded breakfast, she carefully tiptoed across the room and added some small pieces of wood to the glowing embers in the fireplace, before swinging the large iron pot full of water over it.

Then, with a last cautious glance at the still-sleeping James, she picked up one of the water buckets and left the cabin.

It was cold outside too, but the rising sun gave promise of warmth to come. Elspeth took a deep breath of the crisp air, feeling her spirits lighten. It was going to be a gorgeous day and she was on her way to a gorgeous future. Just as soon as she fed the chickens, drew the water and cooked their breakfast. A lighthearted laugh escaped her. That old saying about a woman's work never being done certainly applied to revolutionary times. At least she got to escape in two months.

Grabbing the end of the pump handle, she began to vigorously work it. Once the bucket was filled, she went to the barn to get their feed. Filling an empty coffee can with the grain, she took it and her bucket of water and approached the wire enclosure outside the chicken coop. To her dismay, instead of being in their nests where any self-respecting chicken should have been at that time of the morning, they were huddled in front of the door.

Elspeth set the bucket down, wincing as water sloshed over the rim, leaving a large wet spot on her gray wool skirt. "Damn skirt," she muttered, kicking its overlong length away from her body. Stepping back, she studied the huddled flock, not liking the gleam in their beady little eyes. They looked for all the world like a lynch mob.

You've seen one too many Alfred Hitchcock movies, she told herself. Taking hold of the door to the coop, she rattled it, hoping they'd move back. They didn't budge.

"Shoo! scat!" she yelled at them. They merely cocked their heads to one side and waited.

She was bigger than they were, she told herself. And she couldn't not feed them. James's promise to let her stay had been traded for her promise to do the work. And she could. She squared her shoulders and resolutely opened the door. To pandemonium. The chickens jumped her, pecking at her feet and trying to claw their way up her long skirt.

"Get down!" She waved her free hand at one particularly persistent bird and it viciously pecked her finger.

Elspeth stared in disbelief at the drops of blood welling up from the bite. Cautiously, she tried to back up, but one chicken started flapping its wings, almost reaching her waist. That was the final straw. With a yelp of defeat, she turned to run, got her feet tangled in the long skirt and pitched backward. Straight into a hard pair of arms which lifted her against an equally hard chest.

Still clutching her can of feed, she burrowed into James's embrace. The cloud of dark hair on his chest tickled her nose and the warm, musky smell of his skin successfully blotted out the fetid aroma of eighteen chickens. It took her a second to realize that all the shaking wasn't coming from her own body. James was also shaking, but fright hadn't caused his reaction. Laughter had. Elspeth tilted her head back and glared at his face. His eyes—looking much better this morning one portion of her mind was pleased to note—were crinkled at the corners and his wide grin displayed gleaming white teeth.

"These—" she gestured with the coffee can toward the chickens and then shrank back against his chest as they fluttered aggressively "—these chickens are man-eating killers. Look at my hand!" She shoved her bitten finger in his face.

"Chickens don't have teeth."

"Maybe not, but they've got sharp beaks and the dispositions of tax collectors."

"Don't be ridiculous," he scoffed. "Chickens are harmless."

"I think they're loyalist chickens," she insisted, "and they don't like colonists."

"What they're loyal to is their stomachs. They don't want you. They want that can of food you're clutching."

"They do?" She looked skeptical.

"Sure. Throw some of it over in the corner of their pen and see what happens."

"What I'd like to throw is something hard on their heads." She flung the seed away from her. Sure enough, all but one of them scurried after it.

"Why isn't that one going?" Elspeth peered down at the hissing bird.

"Even chickens are individuals." James let go of her, allowing her to slide slowly down the length of his body.

Elspeth tensed as she slid over the hard muscles of his thighs. For a brief second, she forgot the chicken at her feet. Forgot everything but the feel of him.

"Are you all right?" He peered down into her abstracted face. "Those chickens really aren't a danger."

No, but you sure are, Elspeth thought, struggling for even a fraction of her normal self-possession.

"What are you doing out here half-dressed?" She looked askance at his bare chest. "You'll catch your death of cold."

"I saw you creeping out like a thief in the night and I wondered where you were going. So I threw on some clothes and followed you."

"Threw on some twentieth-century clothes." She frowned at his jeans. "If I've got to wear this thing," she gestured toward her gown, "why don't you?"

"I only wear dresses on special occasions," he said in mock seriousness.

"How do you feel about wearing a bucket of water over your head?"

"You'd better be nice to me or I'll throw you to the chickens." He chuckled. "You fling out the rest of that feed and I'll fill their water dish."

"Just wait till you get your cow," she prophesied. "Then we'll see..."

"Don't remind me." He grimaced. "Can you by any chance milk one?"

"No, and even if I could, I wouldn't admit it. The farmer gets the cow. I get the chickens."

"Whatever happened to women being sympathetic?" he complained.

"Sympathetic!" Elspeth gasped. "After some of the cracks you've made about women, no woman in her right mind would be sympathetic to you."

"What cracks?"

"Oh, little things," she said dryly. "Like women being hard, and out for a fast buck."

"Well, most of the ones I've known have been," he defended himself.

"Big deal!" Elspeth snapped. "Considering where you found them and what you wanted them for, it's hardly surprising. But judging all the women by the few you've misspent your time with makes as much sense as visiting a convent and concluding that all women are celibate."

"That's a pretty thin analogy."

"But one you ought to be able to relate to," she said sharply. "At any rate, you're much too intelligent to have such a knee-jerk reaction to half the population."

"Knee-jerk!"

"Yes!" She refused to back down. "Women are individuals the same as men and they deserve to be judged as such. How would you like it if I were to judge you on the basis of what Jeffery Marston did to me?"

"I know I'm going to be sorry I asked, but what did Jeffery Marston do to you?"

"Told me he loved me and then dropped me like a hot potato once a woman with more to offer showed up."

"More to offer than you?" His skeptical look warmed her heart.

"Lots more. Her father was the president of a Fortune 500 company. But the point of my story is that Jeffery Marston's actions prove that he was an opportunistic jerk, not that all men are.''

''No, your story proves that Jeffery Marston was a fool. Tell you what. If I stop making cracks about women, will you be sympathetic?'' His eyes gleamed with laughter.

''I don't think the 1770s was a very sympathetic age.'' She yelped as the one renegade chicken flew at her again. ''As a matter of fact, it's a downright dangerous age. Why do we need so many of these monsters? Haven't you heard too much cholesterol is bad for you?''

''We'll thin the flock out as we eat them.''

''What!'' Elspeth stared at him in horror.

''Of course we're going to eat them. Farmers grew their own food, and that included meat.''

''No,'' she said flatly.

''But—''

''I will not eat anything I'm on speaking terms with. Even—'' she glared at the irate chicken flapping its wings at her ''—if the speaking consists mainly of swearing.''

''The period demands—''

''My sense of humanity is making a few demands, too. And I draw the line at murder. You don't bear the slightest resemblance to St. Julian.''

''Who the hell is St. Julian?''

''Who the heaven, you mean. He was a man who killed someone because he wanted to know how it felt.''

''And he got canonized!''

''That came later, but I mean it, James. These nasty foul little wretches are *my* nasty foul little wretches and they aren't up for chopping.''

''What'll you give for them?'' He gave her a crafty look and Elspeth felt a bright curl of excitement twist through her. He couldn't mean... He didn't pursue it, she noted, and she wasn't any too clear even in her own mind how she felt about that. Morally, of course, she was opposed to trading kisses for chickens, but it would be nice to have been asked, she thought wistfully. To have known that she'd raised enough interest in him that he desired her.

"You help me with the cow and I'll let you keep the chickens."

"When? In my copious free time?"

"Well, you won't be chopping off heads, plucking feathers, or..."

"Stop it or I'll throw up all over your feet."

"Does that mean you'll help?"

"Sure, one of those books I got from the library has a section on keeping a cow."

"And you weren't going to tell me?"

"I was thinking about it." A reluctant smile curved her lips at his outraged look. "I hate to see dumb animals suffer."

"Speaking of suffering, when do we eat?"

"Just as soon as I finish here."

"I'll finish." He held out his hand for the half-empty can of feed. "You start breakfast."

His companionable smile suddenly reminded Elspeth of her decision to establish their relationship on more formal, employee and employer terms. "I can handle my own work," she said. To her dismay, her words came out sounding petulant when she'd intended them to sound brisk and professional.

"Did you have trouble getting back to sleep last night?" He gave her a curiously penetrating look, and Elspeth felt a chill of unease sweep over her at his intent expression. As if he were waiting for her to say something. But what? Had he been awake enough to remember that kiss after all? She closed her eyes, fervently hoping that was not the case.

It would be extremely embarrassing to have the knowledge of that kiss hanging between them, coloring their perceptions of each other.

"I'm sorry I kept you awake, Elspeth, but—" he continued doggedly.

"S'okay," she interrupted, wanting to get him off the subject of last night in general, and sleeping in particular, before something she said triggered his subconscious memories. "Besides, I have no intention of taking advantage of you."

"No one has taken advantage of me and walked away unscathed in twenty years."

"Yeah, and it's the unscathed part that bothers me," she said dryly. "You remind me of a motto I once saw."

"Motto?"

"Uh-huh. 'Don't get mad, get even.'"

"And that bothers your educated mind?" he sneered.

"No, that bothers my basic sense of morality," she shot back, wondering what it was that he had against education. There'd been too many little digs for it to be a coincidence.

"Ah, yes, if all else fails, fall back on religion."

"All else hasn't failed," she said tightly. "I haven't tried brute strength yet."

"Do you suppose it's because you haven't got any?" His eyes began to twinkle, losing their opaque hardness.

"No, it's because as a rational adult I prefer sweet reason."

"Hm, reasoning can be sweet if done properly. Now I'm particularly susceptible to—"

"Here." Elspeth shoved her can of chicken feed at him. She wanted to divert him from what had happened last night, but somehow all conversational roads this morning seemed to lead to sex. Her wisest move would probably be a strategic retreat. "I'll let you finish the chickens while I go fix breakfast. And watch out for that one." She nodded toward the black hen who was avidly eyeing her, obviously waiting for an opportunity to attack. "She clearly has homicidal tendencies."

"In about the same proportion that you have imagination," he said dryly.

"People with enough imagination to see the dangers live longer."

"In a state of abject terror," he shot back.

"I refuse to stand here and quibble with you." She lifted her skirts to midcalf length so she could walk without the danger of tripping.

"Good Lord, woman!" He raised his dark eyebrows in mock horror. "You are displaying your ankles, to say nothing of your calves!"

"Stick around, buddy," she whispered. "You may even get to see a knee."

"Knees don't turn me on much, but you're heading in the right direction." He gave her a slow grin that sent her heartbeat into overdrive.

"It's rude to mention sex to a colonial woman."

"But you're supposed to be my wife in the book," he countered.

"Yeah, and you're fooling around with the indentured girl. You...you...philanderer, you," she concluded triumphantly. She marched toward the cabin, inordinately pleased to have gotten in the last word. What she wasn't so pleased about was the ease with which he'd ignored her tentative attempt to establish a more professional relationship between them. Ah, well. She'd worry about it later, she told herself as she pushed open the cabin door. Right now, she needed to focus all of her attention on the unfamiliar task of producing a colonial breakfast.

But despite her intense concentration, the meal's preparation was not without a few mishaps. Not only did she set fire to one of James's undershirts, which she was using as a hot pad, but she also managed to burn herself. Twice. That was two of his undershirts down the tubes, she thought as she sucked the scorched knuckle of her right thumb. At the rate she was going through them, she'd better buy them by the gross. And as for buying things, she needed to go into town and pick up some items that hadn't occurred to her yesterday. Such as burn ointment, she thought looking down at her hands in resignation. Or maybe asbestos gloves.

"I'll put your eggs in the pantry." James pushed open the door and walked past her.

Elspeth frowned as the light streaming in the bare windows caught the diamond glitter of water droplets in his jet-black hair. "Is it raining?" She glanced outside.

"No, I just washed up for breakfast. Is it ready?"

"Uh-huh." She kept her doubts about its edibility to herself. Maybe James wouldn't be too picky an eater. One thing was certain; if he was, he'd starve! She watched him as he crossed the room and pulled open one of his dresser drawers, taking out a yellow knit shirt. Fascinated, she observed the way the muscles in his bare back rippled as he slipped it over his head. She could feel her fingers begin to tingle with the desire to reach out and touch his firm, tanned skin, to slowly learn its texture. Her breath whistled out from between her half-opened lips and she closed her eyes against the unexpected longing.

"Um, Elspeth," James's tentative voice provided a lifeline out of the morass of desire she was slowly sinking into.

"Yes?"

"Would you mind putting some of that ointment in my eyes for me? There aren't any mirrors in the cabin." He seemed uncomfortable asking the favor.

"Of course, sit down." She got the medicine out of her purse. "Do they hurt much?"

"A little. I think the sunlight bothered them."

"Hm." She uncapped the small tube and walked around behind him. "Tilt your head back," she ordered. He did, but as she lifted the ointment above his eye, he jerked away.

"Don't move or I might stab you with the end of the tube."

"Sorry," he said sheepishly. "I think it's a reflex action."

"Well, in you it's a very well-developed one."

"I have lots of well-developed reflexes." He gave her a tantalizing smile that sent a flush over her pale skin.

"I'll just bet you do! Starting with your mouth. Are you by any chance Irish?"

"Bite your tongue, woman. I'm Scotch. Bred and born in Aberdeen."

"You are?" She stared at him in surprise. Why hadn't she run across that fact when she looked into his background? Unless he was teasing her? But why would he do that? "You don't sound Scotch," she said dubiously.

"And how does a Scot sound?"

"You know, they've got lovely burrs to their voices. You sound pretty indistinguishable from the general run of the American population."

"Probably because my folks immigrated when I was two months old. My poor mother had the idea that a new country and new companions would shape up my father."

"Did it?" she asked curiously. Concrete facts about his family had been few and far between.

"Eventually, he killed himself."

Elspeth blinked at his matter-of-fact tone. "That was too bad," she offered, unsure of what kind of a response was called for.

"Not for my mother and me. Would you mind getting on with this? I'm getting a crick in my neck."

"Sorry." She allowed the conversation to end, more concerned with getting the medication in his eyes before he changed his mind about accepting her help. Taking a deep breath, she grasped his chin in her hand and braced the top of his head against her breasts. The stubble from the overnight growth of his beard scraped over her palm, implanting tiny darts of sensation in her skin while her breasts swelled longingly beneath the tantalizing pressure.

Eager to end the torture, Elspeth hastily squeezed the clear ointment into his slightly reddened eyes and then stepped back. "There," she said brightly. "Better?"

"A little." He blinked rapidly.

Elspeth sat down across from him. Scooping out a minute portion of the cereal for herself, she handed him the bowl before taking one of the pieces of toast.

"What is this?" He peered at the steaming cereal, his vision blurred by the ointment.

"Cornmeal mush. I'm afraid it has a few lumps. Actually, it has a lot of lumps," she admitted honestly. "I think I put the cornmeal in too fast. Tomorrow I'll try adding it in a thin, steady stream."

"Why don't you try adding it to the garbage?" He picked up the serving spoon, watching in fascination as the pale yellow mixture dropped back into the bowl in sticky blobs. "Unless you happen to like this stuff?"

"Don't be ridiculous."

"Then why'd you cook it?"

"Because the average farm family had it for breakfast."

"What else did they have?"

"Tea and bread or toast."

"No," he said flatly.

"They did too. I—"

"I'm not doubting your facts. I'm simply saying it won't do."

"Well, the book also said that occasionally the adults had a bit of sausage or bacon or leftover fried potatoes, but we don't have any leftovers and modern bacon and sausage are different from what they had. Our version needs refrigeration and while that springhouse may work fine for milk and dairy products, I don't want to risk storing meat in it."

"Even if you were to add bacon to this, it still wouldn't be a balanced meal. You can't spend the morning working with only that in your stomach." He gestured disparagingly toward the mush.

"Why don't you go scramble some of those eggs I just gathered. Then I want to go into town. You'll have to drive."

"All right," Elspeth agreed, rather surprised at his emphatic reaction. While he was right that the mush was totally unappetizing and probably not all that nutritious, it certainly wasn't going to do her any harm over a two-month period. And what did he want to get in town anyway? she wondered. Well, she'd find out soon enough, she decided, and she could use the opportunity to get him some more undershirts. At the rate she was making inroads into his wardrobe, he'd soon be naked. A soft, dreamy smile curved her lips as her mind painted a clear picture of him. His broad chest covered with a cloud of crisp black hair growing down past a narrow waist and over a flat stomach to...

Elspeth Fielding, you're out of your tiny little mind. She banished her memories and reached for a bowl to break the eggs into.

"I'm not wearing this costume into town, James." She suddenly remembered her dress as she almost tripped over the long skirt.

"I didn't expect you to," he said mildly. "I'm doing research, not setting you up as something for people to talk about."

Now that was interesting. Elspeth pondered his answer as she began to beat the eggs with a fork. She would have expected him to have disdainfully ignored other people's opinions, but it would appear he didn't.

"Besides, I haven't the slightest intention of wearing mine outside the cabin, either," he added.

"You've got a costume?"

"Sure, leather breeches and a linen shirt."

"Leather pants?" she repeated.

"Buckskin. They were very common. Why?"

"Oh, nothing." She bent her head to hide her grin. Just wait till he tried on those pants. Leather was not one of nature's more comfortable fabrics, especially if he happened to work up a sweat.

Eight

Elspeth pulled into the parking lot beside the county offices. But before she could park the truck, James emerged from the building and walked swiftly toward her.

Elspeth frowned at the sight of the dark glasses he was wearing. His eyes must be bothering him, because he certainly wasn't wearing them for protection against the sun. She glanced up at the sullen gray clouds threatening rain.

"You're late!" he said accusingly, climbing into the passenger seat and slamming the door behind him.

Elspeth glanced at the digital clock on the dashboard. "Only ten minutes."

"When I told you to be here at eleven, I expected you to be here at precisely eleven," he growled.

"Past grievances," Elspeth muttered, putting the truck into reverse.

"What?" he snapped.

"I was reminding myself of the rules for conducting a fight."

"Rules? You don't have rules for fights. Turn left and go up to the fourth light. Then turn right. We've one more stop."

"Okay." She pulled into the road. "And you do too have rules."

"Such as?"

"Such as it would be bad form for me to remind you that you kept me waiting a lot longer than ten minutes when you picked me up at the airport."

"Nice of you not to mention it," he said dryly.

"You're welcome." She gave him a wide grin. "And I'll tell you a second rule. Never skirt an issue. State precisely what's annoying you."

"I did. You were ten minutes late."

"Regrettable, but hardly worth getting excited about. Are your eyes bothering you?" She shot him a quick, assessing glance. Something that she very much feared was pain had carved deep lines in his lean cheeks.

"A little," he conceded. "The county agent shares his office with six smokers. It really irritated my eyes."

"I can imagine," Elspeth sympathized. "And my not being there when I said I would was the last straw. I would have been, but after I ran my errands I noticed a beauty parlor which took walk-ins. So I walked in."

"Why would you want to do that? You look great the way you are."

Elspeth's eyes widened in shock at his matter-of-fact words. Was that really how he saw her? There was no way to be sure without asking and that would sound impossibly conceited. With an effort, she forced a prosaic response.

"Thanks, but I reeked of wood smoke, and washing your hair without running water is not an easy task."

"I didn't have much trouble."

"You haven't got much hair either. As a matter of fact, did you know that men's haircuts are becoming fashionable for women?"

"Not *my* women!" James's emphatic voice left no room for discussion, and Elspeth stole a quick glance at his set features. Was that a general comment or was he classifying her as his woman? The very thought brought a warmth to her skin and sent a thousand erotic images tumbling through her mind.

"This is the fourth light." James's voice forced her to concentrate on her driving.

She turned obediently, and then asked, "Where are we going?"

"Right there." James pointed to the large sign by the side of the road.

"Campers?" She pulled into a free space in front of the showroom and turned off the engine. "Are we getting a trailer?" A flare of excitement pulsed through her.

"What do we need a camper for? We've got a perfectly good cabin."

Good for what? Elspeth thought, but bit back the words. James was paying her handsomely to put up with its inconveniences and she had no business griping. The problem was, she simply couldn't seem to remember he was her boss. Their relationship was much too tangled to be easily forced into a conventional mold. Even though she knew it was in her best interests to try to do so.

"The agent recommended this place and I called from his office. They should have it ready for me. As a matter of fact, they should have had it ready ten minutes ago." He stared at her.

"Rule Number Two in the *How to Fight Manual* is once an apology has been given, the matter is dropped." Elspeth stared back at him.

"But I don't remember accepting the apology."

"Well, do so because storing up your grievances like a miser hoarding his gold will give you ulcers and no friends."

"I do not hoard grievances!"

"Good. Then you won't have any problem accepting my apology."

"I'm not so sure about this fancy method of fighting of yours." Reflectively, he rubbed his fingers over his chin and Elspeth watched their rhythmic movement as if hypnotized. Her breasts began to tingle, their tips hardening into tight buds of desire as, unbidden, the memory of his fingers stroking over them welled up in her mind.

"What do I get out of it?"

"The warm feeling of having done the right thing?" Her voice sounded husky in her own ears and she hoped he hadn't noticed. It would be humiliating in the extreme if he were to notice her growing fascination with him.

"Wrong," he said succinctly. "Doing things for the glow of moral rectitude they engender is strictly a middle-class phenomenon and I am not middle-class."

"I'll say you aren't," Elspeth said wryly. "With the income you get from your books, you must be in the higher echelons of the upper class."

"Class isn't money. Class is measured by things like college degrees, occupation, family backgrounds."

"You're talking about snob appeal, not class."

"Maybe, but we've wandered from the point."

"This conversation has a point?" She opened her eyes in mock astonishment.

"It's no wonder you know all the rules for fighting," he said in exasperation. "You're so aggravating, you probably spend all your time doing it. The point is that I am not the least bit motivated by the feeling of having done the right thing. I want a more tangible reward."

"Such as?" Elspeth asked cautiously, not liking the wicked smile on his firm lips.

"The possibilities are endless. Let me think about it and I'll let you know."

"I'm not sure I want to be forgiven. It could lead to bigger things."

"Now you're getting the idea." He grinned at her. "We'll—"

"We'll go inside before that salesman comes out here." Elspeth nodded toward the thin, middle-aged man watching them through the plate-glass window.

"All right, but this conversation is simply postponed, not shelved. You can't have everything your own way."

"My own way! What have I had my own way?" she demanded. "You're the one who wrote the scenario for this little venture into the past."

"I may have written it, but you're doing a thorough job of editing it. Speaking of which, let's pick up your latest concession." He climbed out of the cab.

She scrambled after him. "Concession?"

"Uh-huh." He motioned her through the doors. "You are about to become the proud possessor of a refrigerator."

"But we don't have any electricity."

"And we aren't going to either," he warned. "That's why we're here. To get a camp refrigerator powered by bottled gas. When I said we'd live like the colonists, I never intended to risk our health with food poisoning. I simply hadn't considered all the ramifications. The county agent was able to suggest a camp refrigerator as a solution. He was also able to tell me that our well would have been tested when I bought the cabin. It's a state law. So you can stop worrying about typhoid."

The salesman approached them. "May I help you?"

"I'm Murdoch. I called about a gas-powered refrigerator."

"Ah, yes, Mr. Murdoch. As I said, we have two models that would suit your needs. If you'd care to look at them?"

James followed the man and Elspeth trailed along behind, too pleased that she was going to get a refrigerator to complain about being ignored.

"This is our best-selling model." The man pointed to a four-foot model. "It has a freezer and—"

"What about this one?" James gestured toward a small compact unit about eighteen inches high.

"It doesn't have a freezer," the man protested.

"Good, no temptation."

"And it only holds 1.7 cubic feet; whereas, this one—" He put his hand on the larger model.

"We'll take the small one," James interrupted his spiel.

"But with adequate credit, we can arrange low monthly installments," the man persisted.

"I like the small one. It's cute." Elspeth ended the man's pitch before James was able to do so in a less polite manner.

"As you wish." The man shrugged, as if disclaiming all responsibility. "Do you need gas to go with it?"

"Yes, and a spare container." James handed the salesman an American Express card and the man's eyes widened at its platinum color.

"Are you sure you want the small one?" He tried one last time.

"Quite," Elspeth said. "If you'll load it onto the truck, we'll be off. We're in a bit of a hurry." She glanced at James's compressed lips. She was almost certain that his eyes were bothering him a lot more than he was admitting. She wanted to get him home and put some medicine in them.

"As you wish." The man walked over to the counter and began processing the charge.

"Speaking of upper-class," Elspeth whispered to James, "where did you get a platinum American Express card? I've never even seen one before."

"Anyone can get one. All you need is a few million dollars."

"Oh, is that all?" she said dryly.

"No, you also need a way to earn it. Maybe when you write your book—"

"I am not writing a book!"

"Sorry." He shrugged. "It just slipped out."

"Well, slip it right back in before I'm tempted to hit you over the head with it."

"Let me give you a new rule for fighting. Never hit someone bigger than you are."

"Physical violence never solves anything," she said primly.

"That is a fallacy propagated by the weak."

"Oh, I don't know. I'm not very strong and I'm surviving."

"Not very well, or you wouldn't be here in the first place," he said triumphantly.

"Yes, but—"

"Mr. Murdoch, if you would sign this, please."

Elspeth followed along behind James as he walked to the counter, frustrated by the exchange. She could hardly tell him why she was here. Not yet. She frowned, wondering how he was going to take the news of her projected interview. Not well, she guessed. He was such a strange mixture of cynicism, kindness, boyish enthusiasm and what she was beginning to suspect was willful blindness. Conveying the complexity of his personality to her readers was going to be a challenging task. Maybe too challenging. The fear seeped into her mind that maybe she really didn't have the talent to be a topflight journalist.

"Come on, Elspeth. Don't dawdle," James ordered, the smile on his lips robbing the words of their sting. "I want to get home."

"Me, too." An inexplicable feeling of lightheartedness seeped through her at his casual reference to the cabin as home.

"Mike will put the unit in your pickup for you." The salesman handed James his receipt. "You shouldn't have any trouble getting it into your camper. It's not heavy."

As it turned out, the salesman was right. James easily lifted the tiny refrigerator out of the back of the truck. Elspeth picked up the two containers of gas and followed him into the cabin.

"Where do you want it?"

"In the pantry, please. I'll get it working while you go lie down."

"You!"

"Yes, me. I may not be a writer, but I can read just fine and the salesman gave us an instruction book."

"But—"

"But nothing," Elspeth said firmly. "I appreciate your carrying it in. That was beyond me."

"I'm beginning to think nothing is beyond you," he said reflectively.

"But I can take it from here." She ignored what she suspected was an insult. "After all, it's what you pay me for. Now scat."

"Did anyone ever tell you you have a domineering personality?"

"You'd certainly be an authority."

"Women!" he muttered in exasperation. "Always wanting the last word."

"No, really?"

James gave her a baleful look but, to her relief, he left and a few seconds later she heard the rustling sound of his lying down on his straw mattress. A feeling of satisfaction filled her. She'd take her time hooking up the gas and, with luck, he'd fall asleep.

Unfortunately, James didn't seem inclined to sleep. When she snuck into the main room fifteen minutes later, he was lying on his stomach scribbling on a yellow notepad.

Squelching an impulse to grab it out of his hands and demand that he rest, she calmly began to fix lunch. James had hired her as his housekeeper, not his mother. She slapped the sirloin steak she'd bought down on the iron trivet and placed it over the glowing coals.

"Did the colonists broil steaks?" he asked.

"I don't know." She began to shred lettuce into the huge maple bread bowl. "But on the other hand, I don't know that they didn't."

"I take it this comes under the heading Ignorance is Bliss?"

"No, under the heading of ignorance is a good meal. I was planning on thoroughly reading the sections on cooking this afternoon. I'll check then."

"Before you do that, I'd like to work on my book. You did say you could take shorthand?"

"If you keep it moderately slow. My typing is much better. I'm sure you'll find me satisfactory."

"I already do," he said cryptically. "In totally unexpected ways."

And what did he mean by that, Elspeth wondered, but there was no answer to be read in his face. Turning back, she checked the steak. Honestly, James Murdoch could be the most enigmatic man at times. Perhaps, if she hurried with lunch, she could find time to jot down a few notes about him before their working session this afternoon.

But despite her efforts to hurry, the unfamiliarity of doing dishes without running water slowed her substantially and she wasn't done until almost one o'clock.

"Are you finished?" James asked the second she returned from emptying the dishwater outside.

"Yes." She let her breath out in a long sigh. "I most definitely am finished."

"Elspeth." He eyed her worriedly. "Maybe you ought to let me—"

"Listen, my friend, complaining is the inalienable right of every worker. It doesn't mean I'm about to collapse."

"You're sure?"

"Positive, and, if you don't stop jumping on my every gripe, I'm going to retaliate by being disgustingly cheerful."

"How can being cheerful be disgusting?"

"Believe me, it can," she said in heartfelt tones. "Toni used to bounce out of bed at five in the morning, give me this obscene grin and rush off to jog."

"Tony?" James's voice hardened slightly, but Elspeth, caught up in her memories, didn't notice.

"Antoinette Mallory. One semester of her, and I was ready to run screaming into the sunset. Fortunately, the university let you change roommates in January and by that time I'd met Cl—Clarissa." Elspeth caught herself just in time. Claudia wasn't that common a name. As sharp as James was, he'd be bound to wonder, and she most emphatically didn't want to make him suspicious. His normal tendency to delve into people's minds and motivations was bad enough. If he thought he had cause... She barely suppressed a shudder.

"Clarissa...Clarissa..." James murmured. "That has possibilities."

"For what?"

"For the name of the main female character in my book." He wrote something down on his notepad, rubbed his eyes and then stared blankly at the wall. "I picture her as a blonde with blue eyes."

"The eternal masculine fantasy," Elspeth said tartly, wondering if the blue-eyed blonde represented his own idealized woman. The thought unexpectedly depressed her. His heroine probably had overdeveloped mammary glands, too. Men! She stalked toward the stairs.

"Where are you going?"

"Upstairs. To rest a minute. Even the colonists were entitled to a break now and then," she snapped, not even sure in her own mind just why she was so annoyed. So he was enamored of blondes. So what? It had nothing to do with her. All she wanted was the facts; she didn't want to get involved with them.

"I don't know about the colonists, but you can rest whenever you feel the need, Elspeth," he said calmly.

"Thanks," she muttered, taking exception to the very reasonableness of his voice. What was the matter with her? she wondered uneasily as she sprinted up the stairs. She'd always thought of herself as an even-tempered, rational individual who responded to situations logically. But there was nothing logical about her response to James Murdoch. Getting irritated because James made his heroine a blue-eyed blonde was the height of something—probably stupidity.

She flopped down on her bed, rolled over on her back and stared at the ceiling. She was too close to her subject, she decided. She needed to step back and distance herself, both physically and emotionally.

It wouldn't be an easy task, she realized. The cabin was so small as to be claustrophobic and, while she had her own tiny loft, it was unheated and once the sun set, it was freezingly cold, which effectively ruled it out as a nighttime retreat.

So her only viable option was to distance herself emotionally. To build a wall between them. She grimaced, remembering her abortive attempt to establish a more professional relationship this morning. The problem was, he didn't seem to be aware of her efforts. Or else he was ignoring them. She frowned thoughtfully. But why would he care one way or the other? When all was said and done, she was simply the hired help and why should he care what the hired help thought?

She sighed, chewing her lower lip. It was all very confusing. The James Murdoch she was dealing with bore only a superficial resemblance to the James Murdoch she'd read about. So which was the real James Murdoch? The playboy-turned-recluse or the highly complicated man she was coming to know. *And desire.* The words popped into her mind, and she shifted restlessly as the memory of his kiss surfaced, bathing her in a warm glow of remembered pleasure.

She did desire him. She faced the fact squarely. She didn't understand it. Nor did she like it, but to deny it was futile. She wanted James Murdoch. Wanted him in the most elemental way possible—not that she was going to do anything about that wanting. To do so would be tantamount to emotional suicide and she had no taste for self-immolation. Even supposing he were susceptible to her charms, such as they were. And so far she'd seen no real evidence that he found her particularly attractive. The kiss which had shaken her to the depths of her being hadn't even woken him up. If he remembered anything, he probably thought he'd been dreaming. Dreaming of some blue-eyed blonde. She grimaced. Actors were supposed to regularly fall in love with their leading ladies. Did authors fall in love with their heroines? It was a sobering thought. How could she compete with someone who wasn't even real?

And how could she be stupid enough to even consider it? she berated herself. You are here to get an interview so you can get a job as a journalist. But, somehow, her dream of being a reporter seemed to be slipping away from her. This place is just getting to you, she told herself. That's all. Once she got her interview written, everything else would fall into place. And the sooner she got busy helping James with his book, the sooner she would be free to escape from the overwhelming force of his personality. Determinedly, she changed into her period gown and went back downstairs.

"I thought you were resting." James looked up from his notes.

"I guess I wasn't tired. Why don't we work on your book instead? You dictate and I'll write."

"You're on. You're also dressed for the part."

"Which is more than I can say for you. I thought we were in this together."

"It's beginning to look that way," he murmured. "All right, turn your back while I change."

"Sure." Elspeth wandered over to the fire and added a couple of logs, trying to pretend that she wasn't flustered at the thought of his undressing in the same room. She shouldn't be. She poked the fire, watching distractedly as the sparks flew up the chimney. She wasn't some naive teenager who didn't know the facts of life. She froze at the sound of his jeans being unzipped and her breathing shortened as, out of the corner of her eye, she saw them land on a chair. She closed her eyes, and, unbidden, the memory of his broad chest, covered with dark hair, and his powerful thighs filled her mind.

She touched the tip of her tongue to the center of her upper lip and tried to regulate her erratic breathing.

"Good Lord," James muttered. "I'm not so sure about this."

"About what?" Elspeth turned around, her eyes widening at the sight of him.

"What do you think?" he asked.

Thinking wasn't the problem, it was what she was feeling, she thought, hoping he'd attribute the flush warming her cheekbones to the heat of the fire and not to the sensual awareness it really was.

"You look very...very..." Her flush deepened as her eyes lingered on the powerful thrust of his thighs through the skintight leather breeches. "Period," she finally said.

"I feel like these damned pants are about to put a period to my masculinity," he muttered.

"James Murdoch!" she gasped, wavering between laughter and the outrage she suspected she should feel. Laughter won, bubbling out of her.

"This isn't funny! Not only are these blasted pants too tight, but they stick."

"But on average, whoever supplied the costumes was right on target. Mine's too big and yours is too small." She giggled.

"Heartless wretch."

"I'm not the one shouting authenticity from the rooftops."

"After this maybe I'll simply grumble from the front porch." He gingerly sank down on one of the two kitchen chairs. "Come on, let's get started."

"Sure." Elspeth sat down across from him. "Is the muse on you?"

"No, the pants are." He shifted restlessly.

"Be serious."

"How can I be serious with you blathering about muses?"

"So I read the wrong interviews," she excused herself. "Now, what are we doing first?" She picked up her pencil and paper.

"I think character sketches. We'll start with the main one." He frowned, and thoughtfully rubbed the tips of his fingers along his jawline. Mesmerized, she watched the movement, remembering the feel of those caressing fingers. She tightened her grip on the pencil and refocused on the glowing fire, but its radiating heat simply fed the heat burning in her abdomen.

"...think?" James's question penetrated her absorption and she hastily turned back to him.

"What?"

"Are you sure you don't need a rest?" He studied her critically. "You can't be used to expending this much physical energy. There's no reason why you shouldn't ease into things."

"I wasn't tired. I was simply thinking," she said, warmed by his concern. "Now, what did you say?"

"I was asking you for the woman's point of view on my hero. Close your eyes and visualize the perfect man."

Elspeth obediently closed her eyes only to find James's image firmly imprinted on her eyelids. No, she rejected it. James wasn't the perfect man. He was full of flaws. She forced her mind back to the time before she'd known him. It took a great deal of effort, but she persisted.

"He's tall, about six four," she said slowly.

"Washington was considered a giant at six two. Most colonial men were my height or shorter."

"You didn't ask for accuracy, you asked for my image of the perfect man. Now, do you want to know or not?"

"Go on."

"With sun-streaked brown hair and gray eyes."

"Gray! How many people you know have gray eyes?"

"Don't bother me with facts. My hero has gray eyes. He's strong without being muscle-bound. Sophisticated, debonair, witty, kind of a cross between Cary Grant and David Niven."

"You mean a typical Harvard graduate," James said acidly.

"Obviously, you haven't been on the Harvard campus in a while," Elspeth said dryly.

"But your hero has a degree."

"My hero is educated," she corrected. "And a college degree doesn't necessarily signify an education. Just as the lack of one doesn't mean the person is uneducated."

"No?" he said skeptically.

"No," Elspeth repeated firmly, wondering why he had such a hang-up about formal education. As smart as he was, he could have gotten a degree if he'd wanted one. "Education is a state of mind, a constant searching and questioning of the world around you."

"Very few people would agree with you."

"Most educators would."

"I doubt it, but that's beside the point. Take this down." He launched into a description of his main character.

To Elspeth's relief, she had no trouble keeping up with his dictation. It was clear, concise and very well-ordered. Exactly what she was coming to expect from him.

Nine

You can't do that!"

"Hm?" James blinked and stared blankly at Elspeth as if having trouble refocusing on the present. "Can't do what?"

"Can't kill Mary off."

"Of course I can. She's served her purpose as far as the book's concerned."

"You mean as far as that twerp of a hero of yours is concerned," she said scathingly. "What kind of a life have you given this poor kid? First, she's orphaned, then she's bound over by the magistrates to be worked like a slave under the guise of learning to run a household, then she dies in childbirth a month short of her eighteenth birthday. What did she ever get out of life?"

"The pleasure of conceiving the baby?"

"Considering what a self-centered twerp your hero is, I doubt he thought much beyond his own immediate gratification."

"That's not true, and my central character is not a twerp." His voice sharpened.

"Yes he is," Elspeth insisted, ignoring the rest of his response. She didn't need a discussion centered around sexual prowess, even that of a fictional character. "Your hero is self-centered and bone-selfish."

"My hero is a highly motivated patriot."

"Maybe in the big picture he's all right," Elspeth conceded. "But let me tell you, my friend, on an interpersonal level this guy's a nonstarter. He acquires his wife for reasons that have nothing to do with love—"

"In common with most of the rest of his contemporaries."

"And then proceeds to practically push her into prostitution with the commanding officer of the resident British garrison simply to further his own ends."

"But his motives are pure," James insisted. "He's trying to win freedom for America."

"I have never been a fan of Machiavelli," Elspeth said firmly.

"You don't believe the ends ever justify the means?" He eyed her in disbelief.

"Well..." Guilt surged through her as she remembered why she'd taken this job in the first place. "Sometimes maybe, but not when you're using other people. At least," she broke off in confusion, becoming hopelessly entangled in the contradiction between what she believed and what she was doing.

"The strong have always manipulated the weak," James insisted.

"That doesn't make it right. Besides, I thought the men of this period were supposed to protect and cherish their women. Yet your so-called hero is ruthlessly using both Mary and his wife for his own ends."

"Is that how you see a man's role in a relationship? As a refined, educated, bloodless being who puts you on a pedestal and worships at your feet?" he sneered.

"What is it with you and education?" she snapped. "You're always making little digs like that."

"What is it?" he repeated slowly, studying her flushed, indignant face. "Maybe I'm jealous. Jealous that I never had the resources to even finish high school, let alone go to college."

"Well, if that's really it, you don't deserve an ounce of sympathy," she insisted. "You were in the service. You could have gone to college on the GI Bill. You chose not to. It wasn't that you couldn't have afforded it. It was that you had other things to do. And I'll tell you something else, James Murdoch, if it were really that important to you, you'd go back to school now. With your financial resources, you don't have to write these books."

"Yes, I do, although not for the money. Writing books is a compulsion."

"In other words, it's the driving force of your life."

"Maybe once, but—" He broke off as if thinking better of what he'd been about to say. "But you're wrong about my not wanting a degree. If I had a degree—" He broke off.

Elspeth, fearing that he was retreating, tried to lighten his mood. "You'd be exactly the same person you are now. Why don't you get an honorary degree? Lots of people call themselves Dr. So-and-So and all they've got is an honorary degree."

"Lots of people commit murder, but I don't consider that an inducement," he said dryly.

"And adultery, which brings us back to your twerp of a hero."

"Central character," James corrected. "And I'm not going to change him one iota. Not even for you."

Not even for her. She pondered his choice of words, but there was no way to ask him what he'd meant without sounding as if she was fishing for a compliment. And she wasn't here to get compliments, she reminded herself. She was here to help him research his book—and to get her own long-delayed career off the ground.

"Well, if you won't change the twerp, how about if you change poor Mary's fate? She doesn't have to die, does she? I mean she loves him. God only knows why, but she does. Surely her love deserves a happier ending?"

"But love quite often doesn't have a happy ending," James insisted. "My mother loved my father through seventeen years of pure, unadulterated hell. The majority of that time he was drunk, and those were the good times because when he was sober his aim was better."

"Aim?"

"My late, unlamented father was a firm believer in the benefits of physical intimidation."

"You mean he beat you?" Elspeth's eyes widened in horror.

"Until I reached puberty and began to develop physically." James's lips twisted in bitter remembrance. "Like most bullies, he folded at the first sign of retaliation."

"I see," Elspeth said slowly, wondering what kind of monster would beat a defenseless child, and what kind of woman would let him do it, but she kept her observations to herself. It was obvious from his tone of voice that

James loved his mother and didn't blame her for failing to protect him. Maybe there was more to it than his brief tale had revealed. One thing was becoming clear, though; given his background, it was hardly surprising he'd gone overboard on the side of self-indulgence when he'd hit the bestseller list. What was surprising was that he'd had enough common sense to pull himself out of such a self-destructive life-style.

"It's no wonder you've got such a cynical view of life," she said slowly.

"And that you've got such a naive view of authors," he said in exasperation. "This book doesn't reflect my beliefs. It reflects the characters' beliefs."

"That's a cop-out."

"That's the truth."

"Yes, but—"

"Look at it this way. At least we've put Mary out of her misery and, speaking of putting things out of their misery, those chickens are making a lot of noise."

Elspeth listened. He was right. They were making a lot of noise.

"Maybe there's a fox in the henhouse," she said hopefully.

"Aren't you going to go see?"

"Nope." She shook her head. "I like foxes."

"But this morning you were insisting that they not be killed."

"Wrong. I was insisting that I wouldn't kill them. Or eat them," she added at his calculating look. "But, if a fox gets in the coop... Well, it's not my fault."

"That's the most convoluted logic I've ever heard," James said in exasperation.

"It makes sense to me," she insisted. "Although I suppose that noise simply means that the little monsters are hungry. We've been working for hours. I'd better feed them.'' She reluctantly got to her feet.

"And I'll look into what the colonists ate while you do that.'' James reached for one of the thick books from the library and opened it to the index.

Suppressing a feeling of regret that he hadn't offered to go with her, she got up to leave. As she took a step, she got her feet tangled in the clinging folds of her long skirt and pitched sideways. Dimly, she heard the clatter of a chair overturning as she frantically grabbed for the edge of the table to break her fall. She missed, but James didn't. His fingers closed around her upper arm and he jerked her backward against his broad chest.

Elspeth clutched the loose folds of his linen shirt, her face buried in its rough material. She took a deep steadying breath, filling her nostrils with the warm musky scent of his body. An act which did nothing to stabilize her already shaky composure.

"Don't ever do that.'' His voice was slightly unsteady.

"Do what? Fall?'' she murmured, knowing she should move away from him, but completely unable to resist the impulse to remain exactly where she was.

"No, stick out your hand when you do. You'll end up with a broken wrist because a woman's bones aren't strong enough to support her body weight.'' He picked up her hand and loosely encircled her slender wrist with his thumb and forefinger. "And your little chicken-bones are much more delicate than the norm.''

"Speaking of chickens, I'd better go feed the little devils.'' She forced herself to step out of the protective circle of his arms.

"Mind how you go,'' he ordered.

"I will. It's just a matter of getting used to long skirts," she said briskly, hiding her elation at his concern. "I'll be back shortly."

As Elspeth had surmised, the chickens were merely hungry. She paused on the other side of the wire run and eyed them dispassionately, trying not to breathe too deeply. Their water container was still half full, so she simply tossed the feed through the wire and hurried back into the cabin.

She was just hungry, she told herself, refusing to even consider the idea that she missed James's vibrant presence—that away from him she felt dimmer, less alive, as if the wattage that powered her life force had been turned down.

"This book you got from the library isn't any good," he complained the minute she stepped back into the cabin.

"Well, it's better than any you got," she retaliated.

"I didn't get any."

"Precisely. And what's wrong with it, anyway?"

"It has very little actual information about what they ate."

"A common failing of history books. They tend to focus on the big picture." She raked the glowing embers of the fire into a pile and then went to get the food out of the pantry.

When she returned she said, "Why don't you try cross-referencing? Look under things like gardens, farming, general stores, exports..."

"Under the assumption that if they raised it or sold it, it was available to them." He immediately picked up on her line of reasoning.

"You know, what you really need is a computer." She carefully measured the ingredients for corn bread into her mixing bowl. "You could extract all the information from the books, enter it in the computer under appropriate headings and, then when you wanted information about a specific topic, you could print out exactly what you needed to know."

A rising sense of excitement began to build within her as other possibilities occurred to her. "And not just for you and your colonial period. I'll bet there are lots of authors who would like detailed information about various periods of history and would be willing to pay someone else to do their research. Would you?"

"No. Suppose they made a mistake? I'm not going to give the reviewers a chance to point out my lack of education."

"Lack of formal education," she corrected. "Do they?"

"Several have," he said bitterly. "I remember one who said that the caliber of my writing was about what one could expect from a high school dropout."

"Sounds like a bad case of sour grapes from a would-be writer."

"Maybe, but it didn't make me feel any better being held up to public ridicule."

His words dampened her enthusiasm, but didn't entirely kill it. Maybe James's experience had made him reluctant to use a research service, but that still left a lot of other authors who might prefer to spend their time actually writing, leaving the research to someone else. It was an interesting idea, anyway. Thoughtfully, she beat an egg into the mixture and then carefully poured it into a cast-iron pan, put the lid on top and, setting it in the fireplace, carefully covered it with coals.

Lord, it was hot cooking over an open fire. She wiped the back of her hand across her flushed forehead. How did colonial women ever survive the summer? It was bad enough in October.

"What the hell are you doing!"

Elspeth turned in surprise at James's yell. She watched in amazement as he jackknifed out of his chair and sprinted toward her.

"What's the matter?" She had just begun to come to a dumbfounded halt when he reached her and, grabbing hold of her skirt, yanked at it.

"Have you gone nuts?" she squeaked as his large hands succeeded in separating the voluminous folds of her skirt from the bodice. He flung the yards of material into a corner of the cavernous fireplace where it promptly exploded into flames.

"And you aren't wearing your chemise, either!" James's roar of anger was the final straw. She was tired, hungry, overworked and covered with assorted scorch marks, and here was this lunatic ripping off her clothes, and then having the unmitigated gall to complain about her choice of underwear. She did something she'd always vowed she'd never do when faced with an impossible situation. She burst into tears.

"Elspeth!" James sounded shocked. "Don't cry. It's all right now."

"All right!" Her voice rose hysterically. "Let me guess. This precious book of yours has a rape scene and you're getting a feel for it."

"Don't be an idiot." His arms closed comfortingly around her shaking shoulders and he pulled her against his chest. "Not that I wouldn't mind getting the feel of you." His hand cupped the back of her head, holding it close to his broad chest.

The heavy beat of his heart filled her ears, echoing through her mind and breaking the pattern of her sobbing. The warmth of his hard body penetrated her shivering limbs, adding a new element to her emotional distress: an awareness of him. An awareness that was growing to the point of excluding other, more trivial, grievances from her overwrought mind.

Nervously, she took a deep breath as she fought to stem her tears. You're a reporter, she reminded herself. Reporters did *not* burst into tears when the going got a little rough.

But the problem was, she didn't feel the least bit like a reporter. She felt like a woman. A woman in the grasp of a very masculine man. She shifted restlessly and her cheek brushed against the roughly woven linen of his shirt. The action sent a tingling sensation over her skin, and in self-defense she moved her head back a fraction and peered up into James's face, looking for some reason for his inexplicable behavior. She saw nothing in his bright blue eyes except concern. And perhaps...

She noticed the silvery lights shimmering in them, lights she was almost certain had been ignited by the fact that he was holding her half-nude body in his arms.

A feeling of triumph welled within her. James found her attractive. *Her.* A thirty-three-year-old woman who didn't even have a career to make her interesting. But even as she luxuriated in the intoxicating feeling, her normal common sense surfaced, reminding her that she couldn't afford to become involved with James Murdoch on anything other than a professional basis. She simply didn't have the experience to indulge in an affair with him. Even supposing that he wanted one, and there was no sign that he did. Not really. His strange behavior was probably easily explained. Especially for someone who dealt in fiction, she thought ruefully.

"James?" she began.

"Hm?" The hypnotic movement of his hand across her back continued, playing havoc with her concentration. "Are you back to normal yet, Elspeth?"

"I'm normal." She made a token effort to escape from his arms, not persisting when he didn't let her go. "The question is are you?"

"There wasn't anything wrong with me. You were the one with the problem."

"I'll say." She gave him a knowing look.

"Not me! Your skirts were on fire."

"What!" Her eyes widened in horror and she glanced at the corner of the fireplace where her ripped gown was still smoldering, giving off the unpleasant odor of burned wool.

A convulsive shudder shook her and James's arms tightened comfortingly. "But how—"

"Apparently, the hem of your skirts kept brushing against the live coals until finally the cloth began to burn."

"And I was already so hot from the fire I didn't even notice."

"Elspeth Fielding, you'll be the death of me yet."

"Of you! I'm the one who almost barbecued myself, and all because of that stupid costume."

"And a little negligence on your part," James pointed out. "And speaking of negligence." He stepped back and glared down at the thin silk of her panties. "What happened to the chemise and slip I gave you to wear?"

"Why, nothing. They're safe upstairs, which is more than could be said if I'd been wearing the blasted things." She shifted restlessly under his heavy hands, which were firmly clamped around her shoulders. "I guess I'd better go change," she said brightly, knowing she had to get away from a situation that was becoming more explosive by the second. But although her mind recognized the necessity of retreating, her body was unwilling to make the effort.

"Change into modern clothes. We'll forget the costume in the interests of safety. But for the record, why weren't you wearing the chemise?"

"Because it doesn't provide any support," she muttered distractedly, trying to control the uneven cadence of her heartbeat.

"You haven't got all that much to support." His hand slid down over her shoulder to cup her breast. "You're so small and delicate. Like a fairy who wandered a little too close to humanity and was trapped." He rubbed his palm over her breast and Elspeth tensed. The warmth of his hand penetrated the coarsely woven material of her dress and seeped into her flesh, causing the nipple to harden.

"So perfect." James bent his head lower. "You're exquisite," he murmured.

Elspeth gave up all thought of resistance as his lips met hers. Her mind might know she was playing with a fire potentially more lethal than the one consuming the remains of her skirt, but at the moment rationality had no place in her thoughts. It had been drowned in the growing swell of desire his caressing hands were creating. It felt so right, so perfect. As if she'd found the one place in the world where she really belonged: in his arms.

He pulled her tightly against his body, and she opened her mouth to the hard pressure of his lips. Aggressively, his tongue thrust inside.

Elspeth shivered, instinctively snuggling closer to him.

His hands cupped her gently rounded buttocks, lifting her into the cradle of his hips. A surge of heat shot through her at the unmistakable signs of his escalating passion and she clutched his shoulders to steady herself.

A soft sound of pure excitement bubbled out of her throat to be swallowed up by his devouring mouth. As if encouraged by her response, his hand slipped beneath the elastic of her waistband and began to draw patterns across the quivering skin.

Elspeth froze as his fingers slipped lower, closing with firm possessiveness over the heart of her femininity. A flush darkened her cheekbones. She was so caught up in her own reaction that, at first, she wasn't even aware of it when he began to withdraw. It wasn't until he lifted his head, breaking off the intoxicating kiss, that she heard the intrusive sound of a truck in the driveway.

"Ignore it," she muttered, instinctively rejecting anything that would interrupt the intense pleasure she'd found in his arms.

"I'd like nothing better, but I'm afraid it would be a wasted effort." He nodded toward the small window beside the front door. "In keeping with the period, we haven't any curtains."

"No curtains?" she parroted, then blushed as sanity rushed in to replace passion. What was she doing? More to the point, what was she allowing James to do? Hastily, she tore herself out of his embrace and sprinted for the stairs.

To her secret disappointment, James made no attempt either to stop or follow her.

Why should he, you idiot? She grimaced in self-disgust. You've already given him what he wanted. She tore off the tattered remains of her dress and angrily flung it in a corner, then sat down on the mattress. Maybe it was what he'd wanted, but it was what she'd wanted, too; she faced the unpalatable truth with her usual lack of

self-deception. James Murdoch hadn't taken a thing she
hadn't freely given. What really bothered her was the ea-
gerness with which she'd gone into his arms—just like all
those women she'd read about in his newspaper file.
Brainless idiots only too willing to trade sex for the privilege of sharing his life.

Mentally, she squirmed at the thought. Was that how
James saw her? As a woman so starved for affection that
she flung herself at the first available man she met? But
what was the alternative to his thinking that? That she'd
responded to him because he was the man he was? That
was worse, she admitted. It also made no sense. He
wasn't her type. At least, he shouldn't have been.

She closed her eyes, trying to dredge up the image of
her ideal man. She couldn't. James Murdoch had become so indelibly imprinted in her mind that no fantasy
could dislodge him. The knowledge sent a frisson of dismay down her spine.

Yanking open a drawer, Elspeth started to get out some
clothes and then paused as she saw her notebook. Opening it, she began to read the words scribbled there. As she
did, she realized something. Her notes didn't read like an
interview. There was no sense of perspective about them,
no real attempt to delve into his motives. They were simply a dreamy catalog of who James was and what he did.

Elspeth sighed. Ms. Shakely had been right. She didn't
have whatever it was that separated the really top-notch
reporters from the run-of-the-mill ones. That driving
compulsion to pursue a story single-mindedly, refusing
to be sidetracked by things like fascinating men, was
simply missing from her makeup.

Slowly, Elspeth dropped the folder back into the
drawer, feeling as if an enormous weight had been lifted
from her shoulders. By admitting to herself that she

didn't have what it took to be a really good reporter, she had in essence freed herself. There was no longer any necessity to deceive James or to try to force herself to do things she found distasteful. She could forget why she'd originally taken his job and simply enjoy it.

And she did enjoy it, she admitted as she pulled on a pair of jeans. Between setting herself on fire and fending off homicidal chickens, there was lots to enjoy. She found helping James create an authentic, factual framework to support his fictional story deeply satisfying. Much more satisfying than nosing around in people's lives, trying to find out things which were none of her business.

"Elspeth!" James's voice echoed up the stairs. "Get dressed and bring that book on milking you mentioned out to the barn. Silas brought our cow."

"*Your* cow," she yelled back.

"You promised to help," he reminded her.

"Technical advice only. I'm not accepting any responsibility." She yanked the first sweater that came to hand over her head.

"Oh, I accept full responsibility." His deep voice floated up the stairs and Elspeth wondered at his words. They sounded almost... Oh, stop it. She hastily got to her feet. Don't start looking for hidden meanings in everything the man says. Grabbing the book off her dresser, she hurried down to him.

Ten

———

"Did you bring the book?" James demanded the second she emerged from her loft.

"Yes." She held up the slim paperback, using the movement as an excuse to glance at his face. To her unbounded relief, he looked exactly as he always did. There was no knowing smile lifting the corners of his well-shaped lips, no speculative gleam in his eyes. It was as if that explosive kiss had never happened. For a second, pique filled her until common sense routed it. It was better this way, much better. The situation would have been impossible if James had been the type of man to make suggestive comments about what had almost happened—what undoubtedly would have happened except for Silas's timely arrival.

And it had been timely, she assured herself. Her life was in enough turmoil without jumping headlong into bed with the first attractive man to cross her path. And he was attractive. A pensive smile curved her lips. Extremely attractive.

"Snap to, woman. This is no time to be daydreaming. Silas says the cow needs milking right away."

He was also very exasperating, Elspeth thought ruefully as she fell into step beside him. "Then why didn't he milk it before he brought it over?" she asked.

"Her. If it has breasts it's a female." His gaze slowly wandered over the curves visible through her light yellow sweater.

Elspeth swallowed nervously as a still-smoldering spark of desire burst into life, sending a light flush of excitement washing over her pale skin. This was awful! It was bad enough that she was so sensitized to his touch. It would be intolerable if she were to begin reacting as strongly to his words.

"I know the difference between the sexes," she said, forcing a calm reply, "and that doesn't answer my question. Why didn't your cow salesman milk her before he brought her?"

"He says it was to give us a chance to practice." James pushed open the barn door and then propped it open to give them a little light. That was exactly what they got. A little light. A very little light.

Elspeth blinked in the gloom. "More likely he was too darn lazy to be bothered. I swear that man acts like he's auditioning for a stereotyped hillbilly part."

"Auditioning?" James eyed her speculatively. "Have you had much experience with acting?"

"Not unless you count being a bumblebee in the second grade class play as experience," she said dryly. "And if that was a subtle way of finding out if I have aspirations to be an actress, the answer is no. Unequivocally no! I am not an actress or a writer." Not even an interviewer, she thought happily. A feeling of lightheartedness filled her, and she gave him a brilliant smile.

"Why do I have the feeling I missed something?" he mused and Elspeth hastily rearranged her features. James Murdoch was a very astute man. If she weren't careful, he might realize that something about her had changed. And, since he didn't know about either her original plan to write an interview or her subsequent decision not to, he was liable to assume that his kiss was responsible. The thought sobered her immediately, stiffening her pride. She might not be as sophisticated as he was, but neither had she come down with the last shower.

"I imagine you've missed lots of things in your time." She ignored the deeper implications of his questions. "Starting with how to milk a cow."

"As far as I'm concerned, I'd just as soon continue to miss it," he said sourly. "You're sure this is the farmer's job?"

"You saw it printed in the book, and everybody knows if it's printed in a book, it must be true." She gave him a look of wide-eyed innocence.

"Really? I didn't know that." He gave her back the innocent look with interest. "I've got this manual on—"

"You've also got a nervous cow," she hastily interrupted. To say nothing of a nervous housekeeper, she thought, not liking the wicked gleam in his eyes. "Where is it?"

"Her. Her. My God, woman, you certainly require lots of reinforcement on the differences between the sexes. But it doesn't matter, I'm a patient man. She's in the last stall, down at the end." He nodded toward the small window set high in the barn wall. "I thought the light might make her a better producer."

"Producer?" Elspeth cautiously peered into the stall, jumping as the beast shuffled. She hadn't realized cows were quite so big in person. She wrinkled her nose. Or so smelly.

"Of milk." James leaned up against the wooden stall beside her. His forearm pressed against hers and she shivered as she felt the warmth from his bare skin seep through her sweater. "Cows produce milk."

"Yeah, but what kind of milk?" She suddenly remembered something.

"What do you mean, 'what kind of milk?' Cow's milk, of course." He turned slightly and Elspeth's stomach twisted as she felt the muscles in his arm ripple. Gamely, she ignored the sensation.

"I meant, is it safe to drink?"

"It's fresh from the cow. Or it will be if that book of yours is any good."

"It's the library's book and don't beg the question."

"I'm not. I'm begging the information."

"Ha!" She eyed the proud tilt of his head. He was much too arrogant to ever beg for anything. James Murdoch would demand and, if his demands weren't met, he'd undoubtedly attack the problem from a different angle. He was incredibly tenacious. Her sense of unease quickly died as she remembered that she no longer had anything to worry about, because she no longer had anything to hide.

"I might surprise you," James said.

Oh, he'd done that the first moment she'd seen him, she thought ruefully. "What I'm more concerned about is that animal surprising us with tuberculosis. Has she been tested?"

"Tuberculosis? What are you talking about?" James frowned at her.

"Has she been tested for tuberculosis?"

"Don't be such a worrywart." He picked up a rickety-looking stool and cautiously edged his way into the stall beside the cow. "People have been drinking raw milk for thousands of years. Hand me that pail by your feet, would you?"

Elspeth passed over the bucket. "People have been doing stupid things for a lot longer than a few thousand years, but that doesn't mean we have to."

"Tell you what, I'll ask the county agent the next time we go to town, all right? Now, forget the TB, and read me the directions."

Muttering under her breath, Elspeth decided to shelve the argument for now. He was probably right. If there was a problem with infected cows, the county agent would have undoubtedly said something when James had seen him earlier.

She flipped through the book and quickly skimmed the directions. "First, you're supposed to wash its—" she broke off in frustration "—what is this animal's name, anyway?"

"Silas didn't say. What difference does it make?"

"We've got to call it something. You're the author. You name it."

"Mrs. Thistlewaite," James promptly supplied.

"Mrs. Thistlewaite?" Elspeth frowned. "What kind of name for a cow is that? And who's Mrs. Thistlewaite?"

"She was my eighth-grade English teacher. I liked her."

"She'd have been better off if you hadn't." Elspeth laughed. "Now then—" she checked the book again "—you're supposed to wash the udder with disinfectant."

"We don't have any disinfectant. What's the next step?"

"Probably us getting ptomaine to go with the TB." Elspeth sighed.

"Don't be so nervous. We'll simply boil the milk to sterilize it."

"I'd like to sterilize a few of your ideas!"

"As long as that's all you want to sterilize." He chuckled and Elspeth gritted her teeth in annoyance.

"Besides, you don't sterilize milk, you pasteurize it, and we don't have the necessary equipment," she added.

"Mo-o-o!" the cow bellowed plaintively.

"Don't fret, Mrs. Thistlewaite." James patted her flank. "Just as soon as our own little harbinger of doom here gets on with it, we'll get you milked. I presume you aren't advocating that we don't, are you? She might burst."

"She will not. At least, I don't think she will," Elspeth added uncertainly. She didn't know anything about cows and didn't have the slightest desire to learn, either. However, he was right about one thing. They did have to milk her. Elspeth began to read the directions, for some reason feeling embarrassed. A feeling she told herself was ridiculous. They were both adults. But that was part of the problem, she thought ruefully. Her reactions to James were disturbingly adult.

"Reread that first part again while I try it." His matter-of-fact response helped her to control her own embarrassment.

"I don't think she likes it," Elspeth observed dispassionately as Mrs. Thistlewaite stamped her foot and blew her breath out in a noisy stream.

"It's because I feel strange, I imagine." James's brow was furrowed in concentration and Elspeth felt a flood of tenderness at his determination.

"I think I'm getting the hang of this," he announced, his words reinforced by the steady stream of pale, bluish milk hissing into the bucket. "No wonder the early settlers had large families. We could sure use a couple of kids to do chores around this place."

Kids? She stared at his face as in her imagination it dissolved and re-formed into a small boy's, with James's coal-black hair and bright blue eyes. A youthful face without the deep lines that experience had carved. Would he pamper his son like so many self-made men seemed to do? Probably not, she decided. Despite the indulgences she'd read about in his newspaper file, there was a basic core of toughness and common sense in James Murdoch.

"What are you thinking about?" he asked.

"Oh, just that your hero already has one son to help him," she lied. "At least, if you stick to your original outline."

"I ought to. I sold the book on the basis of that story line. That's what the publisher expects."

"Somehow I can't see your publisher's expectations bothering you too much," she said shrewdly.

"Not normally, but in this case my publisher wasn't very enamored of the book."

"Why?" she asked curiously, remembering what Claudia had said. "Everything you write ends up on the bestseller lists."

"Every thriller I write," he corrected. "My publisher is of the 'don't change horses in midstream' philosophy."

"He can't be that dogmatic if he's agreed to publish it."

"He's publishing it, my naive little friend, because I told him if he didn't I'd take my very profitable thrillers elsewhere."

"Oh," Elspeth said slowly. So that was why James was so determined to turn out a book that was above reproach in every way. She couldn't say that she blamed him. It would be a devastating blow to his pride if his publisher turned out to be right and the book bombed.

"Why risk it?" she asked. "Why not stick with the thrillers since they're so successful? Or, if you hate them, just quit writing for a while."

"I don't hate the thrillers. I simply want a change."

"Why?" she persisted.

"I have no intention of boring you."

"Go ahead, bore me," she quipped. "Maybe it'll take my mind off the smell of our friend here."

James gave her a long, penetrating stare and, after what seemed to Elspeth to be an interminable wait, finally said, "I guess it all goes back to right after my second book hit it big. Do you have any idea how much money you can make out of a couple of bestselling books that include book club editions, movies, TV specials, posters, the whole bit?"

"I have a rough idea," she said, remembering some of Claudia's tales.

"Nothing in my background had prepared me to handle that much money and I was like a kid let loose in a candy store, if you'll forgive the cliché. Virtually overnight, I went from living on the fringes of society to being thrust into the middle of it." He paused as if lost in his thoughts; his hands still working with a steady rhythm of their own.

"Rather a heady experience," Elspeth prompted.

"Try intoxicating. I didn't just enjoy it. I wallowed in it. I rented a beach house in Malibu and plunged into sampling everything life had to offer. And then I met Ariadne." A reminiscent smile curved his lips, a smile that sent a surge of envy through her. He never looked like that when he was talking to her. But then, she'd never looked like Ariadne. Elspeth remembered the picture of the gorgeous blonde which had been included in James's newspaper file.

"Ariadne was quite a woman. At least, I always thought so till you came along and I discovered that there's a whole lot more to femininity than sexual acrobatics," he said reflectively.

Elspeth blinked, consumed with curiosity about exactly what he meant. But she wanted even more to find out what had happened behind the bare framework of events outlined in the articles she'd read.

"At any rate, Ariadne introduced me to the wilder Hollywood set and we proceeded to live it up. Or down, depending on your ethics." He grimaced.

Elspeth closed her eyes against the hot, pulsating jealousy which filled her at the thought of what living it up with the beautiful Ariadne had probably encompassed. It wasn't her concern, she tried to tell herself. Her fascination with James Murdoch gave her no right to be jealous of his past. Besides, even if it did, it would be the height of stupidity to be jealous of an affair that by all accounts had been over for eight years. Unless—the unpalatable thought surfaced—unless he still wanted Ariadne? The gossip columns of the time had hinted that the actress had been the one to throw him over. Could he still be carrying a torch for her after all those years? Given James's basic personality, it didn't make a lot of sense, but then men quite often didn't make much sense when they fell in love.

"So what happened?" she said lightly. "Did the financial well run dry?"

"No, I simply found out the truth of that old saying about being able to take the boy out of the country, but not the country out of the boy. My mother could have served as an illustration of the 'poor, but proud' syndrome. We may not have had much, but we still went to church every Sunday and thanked God for what we had. I guess her moral training went deeper than I thought."

"You saw the light?" Elspeth asked, trying to imagine James as a pillar of morality. It wasn't hard. He had the kind of inflexible integrity found in the Old Testament prophets. He'd have been right at home in long, flowing robes atop some mountain, warning the populace of disasters to come.

"No, what I saw were three people I didn't know making love—if you could call it that—on my couch the morning after one of the wild parties Ariadne and I were becoming known for giving. I'm not a prude." He shot her a defensive look. "But neither am I as liberal as all that. To me sex is not a group activity.

"I went for a walk on the beach and took a good long look at myself. I wasn't a pretty sight." He grimaced. "I was wallowing in self-gratification, drinking way too much, living with a woman who had absolutely no appeal to me outside of bed and to top it all off, I hadn't done any work in almost six months.''

Elspeth glanced down at the straw-covered floor to hide the gleam of relief in her eyes. James wasn't still carrying a torch for Ariadne.

"I decided it was time to get my life in order."

"Poor Ariadne," Elspeth murmured, her own fascination with James making her sympathetic to the other woman's loss.

"Don't waste your compassion," he said wryly. "Ariadne had had something going on the side with an elderly French count. When I told her I was going back to New York City to work, she decided to marry the guy. He really suited her a lot better than I ever did, anyway. Ariadne put a lot of stock in things like men opening doors for her, and I've always felt it was patronizing to do something for someone when they're perfectly capable of doing it for themselves."

"Mmmm," Elspeth murmured. While she didn't entirely agree with his casual dismissal of all courtly behavior, she didn't feel strongly enough about it to argue.

"At any rate, my next step was to sort out my priorities. Not surprisingly, my goal at that time was financial security. I wanted to accumulate so many investments that even if I never sold another book, I'd be safe."

"And you did that."

"Uh-huh, about five books ago. But, you know, I've found it isn't enough. I want more than money. I want literary respectability. I want to prove to the critics that I can write something besides potboilers. And I will." His voice hardened with determination.

"M-o-o." Mrs. Thistlewaite, reacting to his tone of voice, shifted restlessly.

"Look out," Elspeth warned, "she's—"

"—going to put her foot in the milk pail," James finished ominously.

"Correction. She has put her foot in the milk pail. Her dirty, germ-laden, heaven-only-knows-where-it's-been foot. I'm not drinking that milk."

"We were going to boil it anyway," he said halfheartedly.

"And are you going to strain it to get out the bits of manure-covered straw?" Elspeth demanded.

"I guess not," James conceded. "I suppose we can pour this out and start out fresh tomorrow." He pulled the cow's hind leg out of the bucket. "Silas said we should milk her at twelve-hour intervals to get maximum production."

"In the first place, I don't want maximum milk production. In fact, she can cease production entirely as far as I'm concerned." Elspeth hurried to keep up with him as he left the barn to dispose of the contaminated milk.

"Dry up," James said. "Cows don't cease production. They dry up."

"That makes two things I wish would dry up," Elspeth muttered under her breath. "And, in the second place, have you added twelve to 4:50?"

"What?" He emptied the bucket and looked around as if searching for a place to set it.

"Here, I'll wash it." She took it and started toward the cabin. "I said, if we follow Silas's suggestion, we're going to be milking that cow at five o'clock in the morning. It's dark at five o'clock in the morning," she added for good measure.

"Hm." He rubbed his fingers over his jaw and Elspeth stared in fascination at the dark shadow of his emerging beard, wondering how it would feel beneath her exploring fingertips. Beneath her softly seeking lips. Against... Engrossed in her imagination, she tripped over the top step on the porch.

"Careful." He grabbed her around the waist, his muscular forearm biting into her soft flesh as he steadied her against him. Elspeth swallowed uneasily as the hard muscles of his thighs impressed themselves on her hips. Giving in to an irresistible impulse, she leaned back against him, reveling in the thrusting heat of his body.

"You okay?" James's voice deepened with concern.

"Sure. I'm fine." She forced herself to move away. "And I'm also right about milking that cow."

"You're taking the coward's way out. We ought to meet this challenge head-on." He followed her into the cabin.

"Your head's certainly hard enough," she said dryly.

"Insults will get you nowhere." He flicked the end of her nose with a gentle finger. "We have to do something about Mrs. Thistlewaite."

"So why can't we do it at seven instead of at five?" She checked her boiling pot.

"Why can't you for once simply accept the script as written?" he said in exasperation.

"Because I'm an editor at heart."

"Are you?" he asked, an arrested expression on his face. "Are you an editor from my publisher here to spy on this project?"

"Great." She threw up her hands. "That was exactly what this scenario needed. Rampant paranoia. Listen, my friend, I am not and never have been in the pay of your publisher."

"Well, you seemed so intent on getting me to change Mary's fate," he excused himself.

"Because I feel sorry for her. I still think she deserves a happier ending than to die giving birth to that twerp's bastard."

"And I still say that love doesn't always end happily," James argued.

"Maybe not in real life," Elspeth conceded, "but you're writing fiction."

"Which mirrors real life. Now, what's for supper?"

"Boiled turnips, beef and potatoes." She began to ladle the mixture into a serving bowl.

"Turnips!" James echoed incredulously.

"Boiled," she repeated firmly. "My book says the colonists ate a boiled meal for lunch. Tomorrow I'll try baking pies and bread and stuff," she offered, seeing his crestfallen expression. "Why don't you wash up while I put dinner on the table?"

"Okay, and after we eat we can work some more on my character sketches."

"After the dishes."

"I'll help."

"You're on." Elspeth smiled happily. She hated to wash dishes at the best of times, let alone with slimy brown lye soap and no running water. Working on his book would be a lot more fun. Unless, of course, he took it into his head to begin using a goose quill and homemade ink. She chuckled at the thought of him chasing after a goose in the hopes of plucking out a feather.

"What's so funny?" He eyed her narrowly. "I've never seen anyone who could laugh with their eyes the way you can."

"Nothing," she lied, as a feeling of companionship surged through her. Somehow, it seemed so right, the two of them working together toward a single goal. A goal that was very important to James. It was strange, but both of them had come up here planning to change the direction of their lives. She only hoped that he was as successful as she'd been. In the space of a few short days, she'd come to a much better understanding of her own talents and limitations, and, even if she wasn't certain yet exactly what she wanted to do with her life, at least she knew now what she didn't want to do.

Her feeling of satisfaction dimmed somewhat as she eyed the translucent cabbage leaves floating on the top of the mixture in the serving bowl. Thank heavens she wasn't hungry.

Unfortunately, that wasn't still true five hours later when she retired to her loft, after having gotten James to stop working by the simple expedient of pretending she was about to fall asleep. Even though she could see a definite improvement in his eyes, she didn't want him to risk straining them by trying to work late in the flickering candlelight.

She set her candle down on the bureau and, sitting on the bed, began to eat the jelly sandwich she'd sneaked upstairs. By the time she finished, her stomach was no longer rumbling, but her fingers were numb with the cold. By November, it would be cold enough up here to freeze water, she thought as she hurried into her nightgown. Ah, well. It could have been worse, she thought, slipping beneath the covers and wincing as the straw pricked her tender skin. James could have been writing about the French and Indian War from the Indians' viewpoint. She grimaced at the thought of trying to live in a longhouse in October.

Although James would have made a great Indian warrior. She had no trouble at all visualizing him standing in a forest clearing. His coal-black hair was held back by a leather band around his forehead that blended into his deep tan. His bare, muscular chest tapered down to a flat stomach and narrow hips which were only partially covered by a leather breechcloth. His powerful thighs were bare, and high, fringed moccasins hugged his well-formed calves. A glowing warmth heated her cheeks and she shifted restlessly beneath the weight of her desire.

Her movement had totally unexpected repercussions as she felt the slight scratch of tiny claws running across her leg. Surprised, she flung her covers to the foot of the bed and found herself staring into the indignant eyes of a small gray field mouse.

She scrambled out of bed and whacked the mattress as hard as she could. To her horror, a second furry little body darted out from a rip in the mattress cover and both rodents scurried down the bedpost. "That's it!" she muttered. Grabbing her still-burning candle, she stalked across the loft and down the stairs.

"What's the matter?" James sat up in bed.

"You want to know what's the matter? I'll tell you what's the matter!" she yelled, her anger making her blind to the fact that the light from the fire behind her was turning her nylon nightgown transparent.

"My mattress is a condominium for mice and do you know why?"

"Is it too much to hope you aren't going to tell me?" The humor threading his voice infuriated her. This wasn't the least bit funny. She could still feel those tiny little claws on her leg.

"Because they are living in that moldy, musty, mildewed straw you stuffed it with."

"That's very good descriptive word choice," James said approvingly.

She stalked over to the bed. "I'll probably catch some horrible disease from them."

"Did anyone ever tell you that you have a tendency toward hypochondria? First you're worried about TB from cows and now diseases from mice."

"I am not a hypochondriac. I am merely cautious."

"You mean you live in a safe, sterile little world where a germ would expire from boredom," he scoffed. "It's about time you emerged into the real world."

"If the real world includes sleeping with mice, you can keep it!"

"All right." He grimaced. "I'll buy a regular mattress for you. In the meantime, you can share mine." He flung back the covers and gestured toward the other half of the double bed. "And blow out that candle before you set something on fire."

Elspeth blinked, completely taken aback by his suggestion. She wasn't sure what she'd expected when she'd stormed down here but an offer to share his bed wasn't it.

Wasn't it? Her emotions mocked her rational mind. Wasn't that what she wanted? Had wanted since the first moment she'd seen him? And, definitely, since the first time she'd kissed him.

Suddenly making up her mind, she took a deep steadying breath, blew out her flickering candle and, setting it on the kitchen table, tried to walk in a dignified manner toward the bed.

Her efforts came to nothing as in her nervousness she didn't notice his sneakers lying on the floor beside the bed. She tripped over them and pitched forward, straight into his waiting arms. He yanked her up against his bare chest. The dark cloud of curling hair tickled her nose and rasped over her cheek as he set her on the unused half of the double bed.

"That's the first time a woman's ever thrown herself at me." He chuckled.

"Ha!" Elspeth made a valiant effort not to let him see how being in his bed was shattering her normal composure. "I'll bet women fling themselves at you all the time."

"No," he said slowly. "Not at James Murdoch the man, only at James Murdoch the bestselling author. But you aren't the least bit impressed by my literary skills, are you? As a matter of fact, you're trying to rewrite my manuscript."

"Just one character," she muttered, wiggling around to try to find a comfortable spot. Now what should she do? she wondered. It had taken all her courage to actually get into his bed. She'd never be able to make the first move, and instead of James doing it, he was turning philosophical on her.

She sighed despondently. Maybe when he'd invited her to share his bed that was exactly what he'd meant. For her to share his bed and nothing else. After all, simply because she found him fascinating was no reason to assume her feelings were reciprocated. She sighed again and closed her eyes, preparing to endure the agony of being so close and yet so far away.

Eleven

Elspeth?" James's voice sounded deeper than normal, and a flare of excitement exploded in her. It seemed he wasn't unaffected by her nearness.

"Yes?" She tried to keep her elation from showing in her voice.

"Are you sleepy?"

"It's been a long day," she hedged, wishing he'd simply get to the point and skip the preliminaries.

"And it's going to be an even longer night, Elspeth Fielding." He paused, and then said, "I would like very much to make love to you, but I don't want to take advantage of you. I mean, you work for me, and I don't want you to think that I expect . . . that I . . ."

"Your hero would simply grab me."

"If you'll remember, you called him a twerp. Repeat

edly. Besides, that's make-believe. You're real. I don't want you to feel pressured."

"Then you should have been a twerp like your hero. Your masculinity is a threat to any woman's peace of mind."

She reached out and tentatively touched his face. The raspy texture of his emerging beard scraped over her fingertips and tiny pinpricks of sensation darted up her arm. Slowly, she traced the crease in his lean cheek. She could feel his muscles clenching under her exploration and his reaction filled her with a growing sense of power.

"What exactly do you want me to say, James? That I find you incredibly attractive? That you're the one who appeals to me, not your literary alter ego? That I want you to make love to me? You're much too intelligent not to have realized all those things."

"Oh, *I* realized them. What I wasn't so sure about was if *you* did, and, if you did, what you wanted to do about it. I certainly know what I want to do. The memory of your wet body gleaming in the firelight kept me awake most of last night."

"You saw?" She winced.

"Don't be embarrassed. You were exquisite. I couldn't believe my eyes when I woke up and saw you cavorting in your bath like a water sprite."

"That tub's too small for cavorting," she muttered.

"And then when I managed to lure you into my bed and kissed you . . ."

"You were awake?"

"Of course I was awake. That kiss would have roused a mummy."

"Then why didn't you say anything this morning?"

"Why didn't you?" he countered. "You seemed to want to pretend it hadn't happened and I was afraid if I brought it up you'd withdraw. I'd have hated that."

Cupping her chin, he looked into her face, lit by the reflected light from the crackling fire. He rubbed his thumb over the soft skin of her lower lip and her mouth instinctively parted. His thumb slipped inside, tracing the uneven line of her lower teeth and the salty taste of his skin filled her with the longing to explore the tastes and textures of the rest of his body.

Her nervousness gave way to desire and she found the courage to blurt out, "Will you cut out all the introspection and make love to me?"

"With the greatest pleasure in the world." James leaned forward and his mouth covered hers.

Elspeth's breath caught in the back of her throat at the contact and her eyelids slid closed, the better to concentrate on the feel of his firm lips. His mouth molded hers with increasing pressure, forcing hers to open wider. Suddenly, his tongue surged inside, aggressively exploring.

An inarticulate moan bubbled out of her throat, only to be swallowed up by his devouring mouth. Her hands clutched his shoulders, her fingers digging into the hard muscles beneath his hot skin as if seeking an anchor in the storm of feeling buffeting her.

She shuddered as he caught her lower lip between his teeth, first nipping and then stroking soothingly over her tingling skin with the tip of his tongue. His fingers speared through her soft curls, holding her head immobile as his tongue continued to explore the warm cavern of her mouth.

Shifting slightly, he flung the covers to the bottom of the bed. Elspeth peered up at him through half-closed eyes. He appeared enormous in the firelight, but she didn't find his size threatening. Not in the least. Somehow, it was reassuring—as if he were a bulwark against the outside world, as if his very presence could protect her and keep her safe. Somewhere, deep in her rational mind, she knew it wasn't true, that security came from within. But right at this moment, she welcomed the illusion. Her excitement threatened to surge out of control as he bent over her, and carefully began to place kisses on the soft skin behind her knee. Elspeth jerked backward in surprise, but he followed, his tongue lightly tracing patterns on her sensitive skin.

"What are you doing?" she gasped.

"I once read that the back of the knee is a very erotic spot in a woman," he murmured, "and I wanted to see if it was true."

"Take my word for it, it is." She twisted restlessly as liquid desire seemed to flow through her blood. She felt as if she were melting.

"James, I..." She gasped, completely losing her train of thought as he gently pushed her onto her back. His fingers seemed to burn into her skin, stilling her agitated movement.

"You're so perfect," he whispered as he began to kiss the satiny skin of her inner thighs.

Elspeth clenched her fists and braced her body against the rough sheet in anticipation as he slowly, methodically began to work his way upward. Yet the explosion of feeling that engulfed her when he reached his goal still came as a shock.

"James, no!" Instinctively, she reached for his head, her fingers clenching his silky hair.

He paused. "But why not?" His hand replaced his mouth and Elspeth stiffened at his delicate touch. His finger slowly, ever so slowly, rubbed back and forth across the moist, satiny flesh.

"I don't—" Her hips lifted against his caressing hand even as she struggled desperately to gain control of what was happening to her. Instead of the warm feeling of shared emotion she'd anticipated, she found herself sinking into a vortex of pure sensation, bounded only by the feel of James's body and the touch of his warm mouth. She found her utter abandon frightening, but her brief moment of hesitation was shattered when James gently slipped a probing finger into her throbbing body. A moan escaped from between her clenched teeth as his action tightened the knot of desire in her loins.

"James, please," she gasped, "I need you."

"And you shall have me," he responded, his voice unsteady.

He slid between her legs and frantically, she arched against him, her last fleeting remnant of sanity defeated by the burning feel of him pressing into her silken flesh.

He slipped his hands beneath her hips, lifting her more fully against him and the throbbing in her abdomen intensified to the point that Elspeth thought she would scream with frustration if he didn't hurry. With agonizing slowness, he advanced, allowing her tight muscles time to adjust to him.

"That's my beautiful Elspeth," he crooned. "Just relax. Relax and give yourself to me."

Frustrated, Elspeth dug her heels into the mattress and pushed upwards, pleasure submerging her as he completely filled her.

"Don't," he said hoarsely. "I want to make this perfect for you and I'm very close to completely losing control."

He lowered his head and caught the tip of her breast between his strong white teeth. Roughly, his tongue caressed the hardening tip until the throbbing in her abdomen became a roar that filled her ears.

Blind to everything but her own overwhelming need, she flung her head back and arched her body upward, straining to take him deeper, into the very heart of her being. Her hands tightened over his hair-roughened thighs in mute appeal.

As if her action had been the final straw, James began to move, pushing forward then slowly retreating before surging against her again. Each thrust of his hard body nudged her closer and closer to the brink of an ecstasy which beckoned irresistibly. At last, with a powerful movement of his hips, he forced her over the precipice and then followed after her....

Finally, after what seemed like hours, the euphoria which seemed to have permeated every cell of her body began to fade and reality rushed in, filling her with doubts. What had she done? She'd made love to James, she told herself, trying to quell her rising sense of panic—made love to James because she was in love with him. The blinding flash of insight made her stiffen with shock.

"Go to sleep, woman," James murmured drowsily, pulling her back against his sweat-damp chest.

Elspeth stared at the flickering firelight and tried to think. How could she have fallen in love with him, she asked herself. How could she have failed to fall in love with him, her mind countered. He was everything she wanted in a man. Unfortunately, he was also a few more things. Her spirits sank as she remembered his status as a literary superstar and his almost indecent wealth. A man like that would never fall in love with a moderately attractive woman on the shady side of thirty. James Murdoch could have his pick of gorgeous young women.

But on the other hand, he must not want a gorgeous young woman, since she'd found nothing in her extensive research to even suggest that he'd been involved with one in the last eight years. Moreover, he had just made love to her as if she were the most important thing in his world. The thought comforted her slightly. Ignore what James might do and worry about what he had done, she told herself. But exactly what had he done? She cast her mind back over the last half hour.

He certainly hadn't taken advantage of her very limited experience to seduce her. In fact, it could be argued that she'd seduced him. She'd been the one to storm down here in her nightgown. She'd been the one to climb into his bed. When he'd asked her if she knew what she was doing, she'd assured him that she did, when in reality, she'd had no idea what she was inviting. Nothing in her past had prepared her for the truth about her own sensuality that James's lovemaking had revealed. It was as if he'd opened a door in her mind, and she'd suddenly found that there was much more to her than she'd ever thought.

She sighed soundlessly, not sure if he'd done her a favor. She'd been ignorant of one whole facet of her personality, but in this case, ignorance might really have been bliss. What was she going to do about her emerging sensuality once their stint in the cabin was up? There was a great deal of truth in the old adage that you don't miss what you've never had, she thought ruefully.

She turned slightly, studying his sleeping form, and a deep feeling of contentment stole through her, helping to quiet some of her fears. Anything as wonderful as what they'd shared had to be right. Somehow, it would work out.

Blast! Elspeth watched in annoyance as the cornmeal mush she was adding to the pot of boiling water began to congeal into large, slimy looking lumps.

In disgust, she ran her fingers through her short curls. Of course, she'd ruined the cornmeal. Everything else had gone wrong this morning. Her gaze instinctively swung to the empty bed, now neatly made.

Where was James? she asked herself for at least the hundredth time since she'd woken almost an hour ago to find herself alone. He hadn't been in the cabin and, when she'd checked outside, she'd discovered that the pickup truck was gone.

Agitatedly she poked the sizzling ham with the spatula. Why had he left? Had he been so dismayed at what had happened last night that he couldn't face her this morning?

Elspeth clenched her trembling fingers into a fist and forced herself to consider the idea. Simply because it had been the most fantastic experience of her life was no reason to assume that James had felt the same way. She winced, remembering Ariadne. Had he compared her to Ariadne's admitted expertise and found her wanting? Had James left to try to figure out a way to tell her he regretted last night?

Probably not, she finally decided. As straightforward as he was, if he wanted to say something, he'd come right out with it. He wouldn't dither.

But where *was* he? In frustration she glanced out the window at the empty parking space. Why had he left? She needed him. Needed him to...

To do what? Her mind mocked her emotions. To tell her he loved her? That last night had been as much a revelation to him as it had been to her? That he couldn't live without her?

Elspeth grimaced at her unrealistic hope. She wasn't naive enough to expect a declaration of undying love, but it wasn't beyond the realm of possibility that he would tell her he wanted her, that he needed her. She expelled her breath on a shaky sigh. She desperately needed some sign that their lovemaking had meant more to him than a quick tumble between the sheets with a willing female body.

The muted rumble of the truck's powerful engine broke into her frantic thoughts, and she turned back to the fire, pretending to be watching their already-cooked breakfast. She might love James with all her heart but until she had some indication from him that his feelings for her went beyond friendship, she intended to keep that information to herself.

"Morning, Elspeth." James entered the cabin with a rush of cool air.

"Good morning." She stole a quick glance at his face. To her dismay, he looked exactly the same as always.

"What's for breakfast?" He peered over her shoulder at the bubbling pot of cornmeal mush.

The crisp scent of autumn clinging to his body filled her nostrils at the same time that despair filled her heart. Last night appeared to have changed nothing.

"What is that mess?"

"Just mush. I wanted to see if I could learn to make it."

Distractedly she set the spatula she'd been holding on the pan of scrambled eggs keeping warm beside the fire. Predictably it fell into the ashes. With a monumental effort she resisted the impulse to kick it. James had made no promises, she reminded herself. She had no reason to be disillusioned by the fact that what had been an act of love for her had been no more than a pleasant interlude for him.

"I have a surprise for you." He gave her a pleased smile.

"A surprise?" Elspeth stared into his bright blue eyes as hope swept through her.

"I hired the teenager down the road to play the part of the bound boy to take care of the animals for you."

"How..." Her voice shook with the intensity of her disappointment. She took a deep breath and tried again. "How nice."

"Elspeth?" James frowned at her white face. "What's wrong?"

"Nothing. I just have an awful headache. You eat, and I'll go for a walk in the fresh air. I need to give Mrs. Thistlewaite some grain anyway."

"But..." James reached for her, but she pretended not to notice. She had to have a few minutes to herself to get a handle on her seething emotions before she blurted out something which would damage their fragile new relationship beyond repair.

Letting herself out, she hurried through the clear morning air to the barn. Once inside, she climbed up the rickety ladder to the loft and sat down in the knee-deep hay, not even noticing the rustling sound as the mice scurried for cover.

Wrapping her arms around her legs, she leaned her head on her knees. "Okay, liberated woman, now what?" she chided herself. "Where do you go from here?"

She could leave and go home to Litton. No, she immediately rejected the idea. She loved James far too much to give up any hope of a future with him without a fight.

But how did she fight for someone who regarded her as no more than a convenience? It wasn't impossible, she encouraged herself. James liked her. He respected her ideas and her skills. It was up to her to nurture those promising beginnings into something more closely approximating what she felt for him. She could—

"Elspeth!" James's bellow came from the cabin porch.

Elspeth scrambled over to the loft window facing the cabin and peered out, wondering what had happened. James sounded absolutely livid. She squinted, trying to see what he had clutched in his hand.

"Oh, no!" She gasped in horror as she recognized her notepad with the information for the interview she'd originally intended to write. How had he found it? She winced at the sight of the raw fury on his face.

With an instinct for survival that transcended rational thought, she sped to the opening in the loft floor and hastily pulled up the ladder.

James erupted into the barn just in time to see the last rung disappear.

"Elspeth Fielding! Get the hell down here," he roared.

Elspeth peered down into his furious features and said, "No."

"Dammit!" he gritted out, flinging the notepad in the corner in frustration. "What a stupid, gullible fool I've been. I thought you really had a headache, and I went looking in your bureau for a bottle of aspirin. I found a lot more than I bargained for."

"Life's like that," Elspeth muttered, thinking of the deficiencies in their relationship. "Listen, James," she began placatingly.

"No, you listen! I trusted you. God help me, I believed you when you gave that touching little sob story about how you'd sacrificed yourself for your poor, old widowed mother. I couldn't believe my luck. Not only were you beautiful and sexy, but you had brains and loyalty, too. But it was all a carefully crafted image you created, wasn't it? Underneath you're just as grasping as every other woman I've ever known. Tell me," he demanded, "was it your own idea to seduce me, or did your editor suggest it?"

She ignored his insulting question in favor of considering his previous words. Did he really think she was beautiful and sexy? Hope began to grow in her heart.

"James," she began urgently.

"Lower that ladder."

"James, I know you're upset, but—"

"Upset!" he bellowed, and Elspeth winced. "Honey, you need to work on your choice of adjectives if you want to make it as a reporter. Upset doesn't even *begin* to describe how I feel."

"How about pigheaded?" she snapped, beginning to lose her own temper. Granted, she'd had an ulterior motive for taking his job, but that motive had been discarded long ago. And he had no reason to call her honey in that sarcastic tone, she thought angrily, as if she were a prostitute he'd picked up for the night and he couldn't remember her name.

"Try wised up! Tell me, how many of the details of our little romp in the hay were you going to provide for your readers' titillation?"

"None. They weren't all that newsworthy!" she shouted back.

"And with your wide experience in 'research,'" he invested the word with a wealth of sordid meaning, "you'd know, wouldn't you? Well, honey, this is one subject who's finished providing you with copy."

"James, will you listen to me?"

"I already listened. And God help me, I was stupid enough to buy it. Right down to that pathetic little touch about your not being able to afford a decent meal."

Elspeth winced, remembering her lie. "It wasn't like that."

"Oh, I'm sure it wasn't," he purred, "but I know how it's going to be." He looked around, and, finding an old wooden toolbox, he dragged it beneath the loft opening and stepped on it.

"James, will you get your mind out of the gutter long enough to listen to me. I have no intention of writing that interview."

She moved back slightly as he grasped the opening and swung his body over the edge onto the loft floor. The emotions seething through him seemed to supercharge the air in the cramped loft.

"That's why you came," he accused.

"Yes, but that's not why I stayed. I found that I not only don't have the talent to be a top-notch reporter, I don't have the drive."

"And what else did you discover?" James slowly began to stalk her.

Elspeth cautiously retreated, trying to gauge his exact mood. It was impossible, although she was almost certain that he was nowhere near as angry as he had been.

"Well, that I'd like to start up a research service. Do you really think I'm beautiful?" she blurted out.

"We're not discussing your looks but your actions," he said repressively.

"*My* actions!" Elspeth exploded. "What about *yours*?"

"I didn't do anything." He looked dumbfounded at her charge.

"I'll say you didn't!" she yelled. "You never said a word about last night. You didn't even wait around till I woke up. You just took everything I had to give and left."

"I wanted to line up a bound boy so you wouldn't have to cope with the livestock," he defended himself.

"You didn't say *anything*, not a single word." Elspeth glared at him.

"Do you think you're the only one who might want to be told how your partner feels," he demanded. "Did it ever occur to you that I might be worried about your response?"

"No," Elspeth replied simply. "You're a complete hunk, and wealthy to boot. Even with your aggravating habits, you're a fantastic catch."

"*I'm* aggravating!" He inched closer, and Elspeth cautiously moved back. "You have a corner on the aggravation market. No wonder it took me so long to realize that I was in love with you."

Elspeth momentarily froze, uncertain of whether he'd actually said the words or whether they'd been conjured up from the depths of her intense longing.

James took advantage and lunged forward, grabbed her around the waist and tumbled her over into the thick straw.

Elspeth shivered with a surge of pleasure as his large body covered hers and he boldly pushed his knee between her slender thighs.

She inhaled sharply as her eyes met his and she saw the desire in their depths. A blinding sense of exultation filled her at the thought that she was responsible for that look. Wonderingly, she began to trace the flush that stained his high cheekbones. Her pleasure intensified as she felt him shudder beneath the pressure of her wandering fingers.

James lowered his head and began to nuzzle the sensitive skin behind her ear, then lightly nibbled on the lobe. A gasping moan escaped her parted lips as his tongue began to outline her ear. The sound seemed to inflame him. His fingers speared through her tangled curls, holding her immobile. Slowly, he began to kiss her with drugging insistence as if he were intent on discovering every nuance of the flavor and texture of her mouth.

The warmth running beneath her skin became a blazing inferno as his hand slipped beneath her sweater, and he cupped her breast, first kneading the satiny flesh and then rubbing his thumb over the hardening tip. Elspeth twisted beneath him as a hot, melting sensation flowed through her, collecting in a tight coil of desire deep in her abdomen.

With an impatient movement James pulled her sweater off and, bending his head, drew the beaded tip of one breast into his mouth while his fingers gently massaged the other. Elspeth whimpered longingly as the tension that had her in its grip tightened unbearably. Frantically she plucked at his shirt, wanting, needing the feel of his bare skin against hers.

James complied with her unspoken request, yanking off his clothes and removing her jeans.

Slowly, reverently, James swept his hand from her shoulder to her thigh and back again. Elspeth trembled uncontrollably as his callused palm caressed her sensitive skin, bringing thousands of nerve endings to singing life.

"You say you want words," he muttered, "but there aren't sufficient words in the English language to tell how beautiful you are. To exactly describe the velvety softness of your skin or the intoxicating taste of it." His tongue flicked out to paint a tantalizing design on the fluttering skin of her abdomen.

Elspeth reached for him, her fingers digging into the muscles of his broad shoulders as she tried to pull him closer. Willingly, he went, carefully positioning himself between her thighs.

A sharp gasp escaped her as he pressed forward. "Ah, James," she arched upwards, intensifying the exquisite sensation, "you feel so...so..." Elspeth's head twisted from side to side as the tension gripping her quickly approached the breaking point.

"It defies description, doesn't it?" His chuckle was slightly unsteady as he clasped her chin, holding her head still. Looking deep into her misty eyes, he boldly entered her with one powerful movement.

Elspeth shuddered convulsively beneath the thrusting heat of his body. "I love you," she gasped. "Love you, love you, love you, love you . . ." Her words ended on a high keening sound as James totally lost control and sent them both hurtling into a mindless void of pure sensation.

As she slowly drifted down through clouds of satiation to full awareness, she heard him mutter, "Damn."

"What's the matter?" She gave him a smile of pure contentment.

"I meant to take my time making love to you," he said ruefully. "I was going to linger over every exquisite inch and then you said you loved me, and I went up in flames."

"I'm glad," Elspeth said in satisfaction, snuggling deeper into his protective embrace. "Since that's the effect you have on me, it only seems fair that it be reciprocated. Besides, you said everything that was important when you told me you loved me," she said, no longer doubting that he'd actually said it.

"Not everything." He cupped her flushed face in his large hands. "Elspeth, will you marry me? Have my children? Grow old with me?"

Elspeth blinked back the tears of happiness that suddenly filled her eyes.

"I'll remodel my attic as an office for your research service," he coaxed.

"You fantastic man!" She nearly cracked his ribs with the strength of her hug. "You don't have to bribe me. I'd sell my soul for the chance to be your wife."

"Thank God for that." He punctuated each word with a kiss. "But forget Faust, I never liked him. Although, you know," his eyes narrowed reflectively, "the Middle Ages would be an interesting period to set a book."

Elspeth blinked in horror. "Absolutely not! The 1700s is as far as I go."

"Really?" His eyes twinkled wickedly. "Let me show you how far I'm willing to go." He gathered her willing body up in his arms.

*   *   *   *   *

CHILDREN OF DESTINY

A trilogy by Ann Major

Three power-packed tales of irresistible passion and undeniable fate created by Ann Major to wrap your heart in a legacy of love.

PASSION'S CHILD — September

Years ago, Nick Browning nearly destroyed Amy's life, but now that the child of his passion—the child of her heart—was in danger, Nick was the only one she could trust....

DESTINY'S CHILD — October

Cattle baron Jeb Jackson thought he owned everything and everyone on his ranch, but fiery Megan MacKay's destiny was to prove him wrong!

NIGHT CHILD — November

When little Julia Jackson was kidnapped, young Kirk MacKay blamed himself. Twenty years later, he found her...and discovered that love could shine through even the darkest of nights.

Don't miss PASSION'S CHILD, DESTINY'S CHILD and NIGHT CHILD, three thrilling Silhouette Desires designed to heat up chilly autumn nights!

SD-445

ATTRACTIVE, SPACE SAVING BOOK RACK

Display your most prized novels on this handsome and sturdy book rack. The hand-rubbed walnut finish will blend into your library decor with quiet elegance, providing a practical organizer for your favorite hard-or soft-covered books.

Only $9.95

Approximately 16" x 8" when assembled

Assembles in seconds!

To order, rush your name, address and zip code, along with a check or money order for $10.70* ($9.95 plus 75¢ postage and handling) payable to *Silhouette Books.*

Silhouette Books
Book Rack Offer
901 Fuhrmann Blvd.
P.O. Box 1396
Buffalo, NY 14269-1396

Offer not available in Canada.

*New York and Iowa residents add appropriate sales tax.

BKR-2A

 Silhouette Desire

COMING
NEXT MONTH

#445 PASSION'S CHILD—Ann Major
Book One of the CHILDREN OF DESTINY trilogy!
Amy Holland and Nick Browning's marriage of convenience could
turn to passion—if the secret of their child was not revealed....

#446 ISLAND HEAT—Suzanne Forster
When Justin Dunne's search led him to a "haunted castle" and
beautiful Lauren Cambridge, he knew it wasn't the right time to get
involved, unless he could mix business *and* pleasure.

#447 RAZZMATAZZ—Patricia Burroughs
Being stranded in the Reno airport left Kennie Sue Ledbetter with
limited options. Alexander Carruthers came to her rescue, and
somehow the next morning she found herself married . . . to him!

#448 TRUE COLORS— Mary Blayney
It would take all of television heartthrob Tom Wineski's considerable
charm to convince small-town single mother Janelle Harper he'd
developed a forever kind of passion.

#449 A TASTE OF HONEY—Jane Gentry
Susannah Reid was content with her life . . . until notorious Jefferson
Cody hit town. He convinced her to start thinking about her own
happiness—not what the neighbors would say.

#450 ROUGHNECK—Doreen Owens Malek
Beau Landry was a direct contrast to refined lawyer Morgan Taylor.
Beau had done the wrong thing for the right reason, but when he
proposed, would Morgan approve of his tactics?

AVAILABLE NOW:

Silhouette Desire

Don't miss the enchanting
TALES OF THE RISING MOON
A Desire trilogy by Joyce Thies

MOON OF THE RAVEN—June (#432)
Conlan Fox was part American Indian and as tough as the
Montana land he rode, but it took fragile yet strong-willed
Kerry Armstrong to make his dreams come true.

REACH FOR THE MOON—August (#444)
It would take a heart of stone for Steven Armstrong to evict
the woman and children living on his land. But when Steven saw Samantha, eviction was the last thing on his mind!

GYPSY MOON—October (#456)
Robert Armstrong met Serena when he returned to his an-
cestral estate in Connecticut. Their fiery temperaments
clashed from the start, but despite himself, Rob was falling under the Gypsy's spell.
